CROOKS

Also by Peter Whalley

Harry Sommers' Novels

Robbers
Rogues
The Mortician's Birthday Party

CROOKS

Peter Whalley

Walker and Company
New York

Published in the United States of America in 1988 by the
Walker Publishing Company, Inc.

Library of Congress Cataloging-in-Publication Data

Whalley, Peter, 1946–
    Crooks.

    I. Title.
PR6073.H35V55   1988   823'.914   87-37267
ISBN 0-8027-1038-7

Printed in the United States of America

10 9 8 7 6 5 4 3 2 1

CROOKS

1.

It had been a long, cold winter that seemed to be turning into a long, cold spring. Though almost Easter, there was still a frost in the mornings and, as often as not, rain by the afternoons.

Harry Sommers clutched his jacket about him as he left the shelter of his car and hurried across the road towards the Oasis ballroom where South Londoners had once waltzed the night away. It was now the New Oasis Cinema Club where they watched 'adult' movies and, alongside it in the same decaying building, the New Oasis Social Club (Members Only) where they could drink till two in the morning.

A middle-aged woman in horn-rimmed spectacles and an overcoat buttoned to her chin sat in the pay-booth smoking a cigarette. She was flanked by pictures of much younger women who wore nothing at all and had their legs spread alluringly.

She removed the cigarette from her mouth as Harry approached. 'Three pounds, please.'

Harry shook his head. 'I've got an appointment with Mr Shapiro.'

'In the club,' she said, replacing the cigarette and directing him to the Members Only door, which had a spy-hole set in the middle of it.

'Cheers.'

Inside, the air was warm and stale from the night before. A stocky, unshaven man was sweeping round the chairs and tables. He looked up aggressively as Harry entered. Me ten years on, thought Harry. Me if the Agency hadn't come along, presenting an alternative to minding bars. He was about to repeat his appointment-with-Mr-Shapiro formula, then saw that Leo Shapiro was already sitting at a corner table and counting money.

He was a large man, near to Harry's height but paunchier.

1

And decidedly more prosperous-looking with a fur-lined coat draped around his shoulders and a display of gold rings and chains that would have put many a jeweller's window to shame.

'All right, Leo?' said Harry, advancing.

'Harry . . . ! Good of you to come. Sit down.'

'Long time no see.'

'Must be a while, yes. Now, what'll you have? A whisky to keep out the cold?'

'Don't mind if I do,' said Harry, postponing again his resolution not to drink at lunch-times.

'Two whiskies, Dave, if you'd be so good,' requested Shapiro. The unshaven Dave put down his brush and went to do the honours.

Harry had first made the acquaintance of Leo Shapiro at the age of fifteen when both had attended the local youth club in Stepney. Then Leo the Jew, as he'd been generally known – not because there weren't other Jews but because he was their natural leader – was already into fencing the stuff the other kids, mainly gentiles, were nicking from Woolworths. Harry wasn't one of them, being more interested in the fortunes of West Ham and the possibilities for under-age drinking. Nevertheless, each remained aware of the other and had retained since a sneaking interest in how the other was faring. Harry had joined the army, boxed and won awards; come out of the army, gone on fighting and got sent down for it. Shapiro had graduated into the import and export business, mainly magazines and videos, and invested in property. Each had sailed close to the wind but had come out – just – on the side of the righteous: Harry, because Clifford Humphries had died of a heart attack and indirectly bequeathed him the Coronet Private Detective Agency; Shapiro, because his early successes had given him a taste for the good life he'd no wish to jeopardise. His clubs and flats might be the haunts of prostitutes and their clients, but Shapiro himself stayed as clean as a whistle, observing fire-regulations, membership requirements and the latest guide-lines that porno movies should stop short of showing actual penetration.

2

They met not as friends exactly, more acquaintances whose lives seemed always about to diverge for ever but never quite managed to. And also as private detective and would-be client. Shapiro had that morning phoned Harry's office asking if he'd mind calling to talk business.

Dave served their drinks and went back to his sweeping up.

'And how's the private-eye racket, then?' Shapiro enquired after they'd drunk to one another's health.

'Ticking over,' said Harry modestly.

'I'm pleased to hear it.'

'Not half as much as I am.'

In fact, the Agency was sharing in the boom being enjoyed by private education and medicine. People with money and problems had been persuaded to believe the one could be used to solve the other and had been turning up on Harry's doorstep with rewarding regularity. In his absence they spoke to Yvonne, his partner and the ex-mistress of Clifford Humphries to whom the Agency had actually been bequeathed. Either way they kept coming, keeping Harry working twelve hours a day, six, sometimes seven, days a week. He'd come promptly in response to Shapiro's call only because he couldn't resist the chance to see the bastard again.

'It's nice to find an East End boy making good, Harry.'

'Thanks.'

'You want to know how I'm doing?'

'No. You'll only make me jealous.'

Shapiro laughed and then, the social preliminaries over, came to the point.

'This Agency of yours, do you do tracing?'

'Of what?'

'People. There's somebody I want to get in touch with. Only he's moved, and I don't know where he's living. Can you find him?'

'We can try.'

'Well, I can do that myself. I can try. But what I want is that you should find him.'

'We can try,' repeated Harry, determined to stand his

3

ground. He felt a need to make clear he wasn't any longer available as muscle for the night and sweeping-up the morning after; he was a man with a profession which, like all, had its secrets.

'OK. So you can try. But I need to contact him quickly.'

'How quickly?'

'Today.'

Harry smiled.

'I'm serious,' insisted Shapiro.

'I'm sure you are.' It was no more than par for the course. Anybody wanting to contact anybody wanted to do so today; nobody ever said they wanted to contact somebody slowly.

'Well, let's say some time within the next few days, then,' conceded Shapiro. 'But no longer than that.'

'And what's your relationship with this person?' said Harry, going by the book.

'I haven't one. My relationship is I want to know where he's got to.'

'I mean is he a relative? Or a friend? Or what?'

'No. He used to be a neighbour. Will that do?'

'Yes. And he's moved away, has he?'

'If he hadn't moved away then I'd know where he was.'

'Do you know where he's moved to?'

'No.'

'No idea?'

'None.'

'How long ago was this move?'

'Oh . . . six months. Something like that. We were next-door neighbours, then early one morning he'd upped and gone.'

'And where was this? Where do you live?'

Shapiro hesitated. It was the in-built defensiveness of one whose home and business lives were never allowed to meet. Then, realising the inevitability of such information, he gave a small laugh at his own caution and said, 'Dulwich.'

'Where in Dulwich?'

'Number three, Waverley Crescent.'

'And the man you want me to find . . . ?'

4

'Number five.'

Harry printed the address on a fresh page of his note-book.

'Let's have another,' said Shapiro, referring to their empty glasses. 'Brass monkey weather, this.'

Dave was again summoned, then Shapiro said, 'Will you do it? Will you find this guy for me?'

Harry nodded. 'All right.'

'Terrific.'

'But if you want it done quickly then it'll mean dropping other jobs. Which will have to be reflected in the fee.'

Shapiro made a gesture of indifference. 'I know you won't try and rip me off.'

It was more a put-down than a compliment; he might have had more respect had he thought Harry capable of ripping him off.

'One thing, though,' said Harry.

'What?'

'If I do trace this guy . . . '

'Which I'm sure you will.'

'If I do,' repeated Harry patiently, 'I can't give you his new address unless he wants me to. When I find him, all I can do is tell him you want to get in touch. After that it's up to him.'

Shapiro smiled. 'You think I'm going to send Dave here to cut him up or something?'

Harry shrugged. 'Nothing personal. It's the way we work.'

'I pay you for tracing somebody, and then, when you do, you won't give me his address . . . ?'

'That's it. People have a right not to be traced if they don't want to be.'

Shapiro seemed entertained by such niceties but wasn't deterred. 'You just find him. And tell him I want him to do a little job. For which he'll be paid well over the odds. And given a free holiday into the bargain.'

Harry wondered for a moment if he were serious. 'You want me to tell him that?'

'Certainly.'

'Right. And what's his name?'

'Buller. Eric Buller.'

'And he moved from number five, Waverley Crescent, Dulwich, about six months ago.'

'Correct.'

'But you don't know where to.'

'If I knew that . . . ' said Shapiro, and smiled.

'You wouldn't need me,' completed Harry for him.

By the following afternoon Harry had Eric Buller's new address and was on his way to see him. Yvonne had unearthed it, working from Yellow Pages through the removal firms of South-East London till she'd found the one Eric Buller had employed and then cajoling them into giving her his new address.

Routine stuff that Shapiro could have done for himself had he a mind to, but then so was most private detecting. Knowing where to look and refusing to take no for an answer were the two most important qualities of any private eye. The hard drinking, womanising and indomitable courage were optional.

Buller had moved northwards to Slough. Fifty-eight, Caledonian Road, to be precise. It turned out to be a late-Victorian terrace, with overflowing dustbins and neglected pavements that suggested an area in decline. One house was boarded up, and another looked abandoned, its door hanging open and windows smashed.

It was raining steadily as Harry parked outside number 58, which boasted a front door with its stained glass intact but with no bell or knocker. He rapped with his knuckles on the woodwork then ducked back away from the small Niagara of rainwater cascading from the defective guttering above.

Waiting for someone to answer, he had time to wonder why Eric Buller had gone from being next-door neighbour to Leo Shapiro – which had to mean somewhere up-market, Shapiro's income being what it was – to this. A coming-down in the world that surely couldn't have been of his own choosing. Then the door was opened by a smartly dressed woman carrying a pekinese dog under one arm.

6

'Yes?'

'I'm looking for a Mr Eric Buller.'

'Who shall I say wants him?'

'Well, I'd like to speak to him on behalf of a client.' And he handed her a card identifying himself as Harry Sommers of the Coronet Private Investigation Agency.

Her manner, never exactly welcoming, became positively hostile.

'Oh, Christ,' she said.

'It's nothing to worry about . . . ' began Harry, seeking to reassure.

'What the hell has he got himself into now?' Taking its cue from her, the pekinese bared its tiny teeth.

'It's an acquaintance who wants to contact him. I'm sure it's nothing to worry about.'

She looked at him, still suspicious, then gave a shrug of indifference and said, 'You'd better come in.'

Harry dodged the downpour and stepped inside. She left him to close the door himself, turned and went away along the narrow hallway.

'Somebody to see you,' she said into an open door, then nodded back to Harry. 'He's in there.' The pekinese snarled its agreement before the woman carried it away to the back of the house.

'Thanks,' said Harry, stepping into a parlour stuffed with furniture, where a colour television set was showing the afternoon's racing. The man watching it had half-risen from his armchair and was looking at him in surprise.

'Mr Eric Buller?'

'Yes.'

He seemed older than his wife, or was it just that he was more careless about his appearance? His baggy sweater and carpet-slippers suggested he wasn't up to much of an effort any more and seldom ventured beyond his own front door.

Harry offered his card and an explanation of why he was there. Eric Buller listened attentively, then turned off the television and invited him to sit down.

7

'Leo Shapiro,' he said, as though finding it difficult to believe.
'Yes.'

'Well, there's a surprise.'

'He said you were next-door neighbours.'

'Oh, we were. For ten years or more. But we weren't close friends or anything. I just wonder why he wants to get in touch.'

'He said he wants you to do a job for him.'

'A job.'

'Reckons he'll be paying over the odds.'

Harry waited, curious as to whether anything might now be revealed about this mild-mannered individual and his unwelcoming wife. Her reaction to the sight of Harry's card had hinted at a recent past that hadn't been a bed of roses. What the hell has he got himself into now? she'd exclaimed. Suggesting he'd been in one or two unpleasant things already.

But Eric Buller only smiled and said, 'Nice of him.'

'He said you'd be given a holiday as well.'

'A holiday . . . ?'

'That's what he said.'

'Can't be bad. And where's this holiday to be? Somewhere abroad, I hope? Somewhere with some sun?'

Harry couldn't tell whether he was genuine or teasing. 'He didn't say. But he did sound as though it was urgent. As though he had to get in touch with you straight away.'

'Sounds even more interesting.'

'Well anyway, my job is to tell you that. Which I've now done. Whether you want to get in touch with him is entirely up to you. But there's no way I'll give him your address if you don't want me to. OK?'

'I understand. But no, I don't mind having a word with Leo. I don't mind at all. Why should I? I'm not exactly rushed off my feet at the moment, am I?'

He spoke as though faintly amused by his own situation: with self-mockery but no self-pity. There was a keen intelligence there behind the shabby clothes and show of idleness that made Harry wonder again what might have exiled him from Leo Shapiro's metropolitan suburbia to the squalor of Caledonian

8

Road. However, he wasn't being paid to worry about that. Simply to deliver a message and, if requested, take one back.

'So you do intend to contact Mr Shapiro, then?'

'Yes.' It was a considered reply.

'If you like, I can give Mr Shapiro your address and ask him to get in touch with you . . . ?'

'I'd have no objections to that. None at all.'

'Do you have a phone number where he can reach you?'

Eric Buller nodded and recited it while Harry wrote it down. Which seemed to conclude all he had come for.

'Well, thanks. I won't keep you any longer.'

'You're welcome to stay and watch the two-thirty at Doncaster if you like.' And he switched the television back on.

'No, I'd best get going,' said Harry. They shook hands, and Eric Buller led him back down the narrow hallway.

Outside, the rain had abated to a steady drizzle.

'It had better be abroad,' said Eric Buller. 'I don't want a holiday in this damn country. Not with weather like this.'

'Bye now,' said Harry, then he turned up his coat collar and hurried to his car.

As he pulled away he saw that Eric Buller was still on his doorstep, watching him go. He raised a hand in salute and was given a wave in reply.

He could have had Yvonne convey the results of the investigation to Shapiro, but it wasn't far to his club in Deptford, and Harry felt an obscure desire to let him know face to face of his success. A phone-call established that Shapiro was normally on the premises between six and eight in the evening. Harry arrived at seven and was nodded through by the lady in the horn-rimmed spectacles.

This time Dave, though still unshaven, was behind the bar. There were perhaps a dozen customers, all men but for one attractive if well-worn red-head who was perched on a bar-stool waiting for someone to show an interest and replenish her drink. She gave Harry a small, encouraging smile, which switched off abruptly when he ignored her and said

9

to Dave, 'Is Mr Shapiro in?'

'Office through there,' said Dave, indicating an unmarked door to one side of the bar.

Harry stepped through, negotiated a pile of crates and came to another, already open door.

'Harry. Come in,' said Shapiro from behind a plush-looking desk the top of which was clear save for an ashtray and telephone. 'Join me in a whisky?'

'Thanks. I will.'

He sat on a leather sofa that faced the desk while Shapiro busied himself with glasses. Then, to his surprise, Harry noticed a small window in one wall through which he could see two naked women making love to one another.

'You want ice?'

'Er . . . yes.'

Noticing that Harry's attention had strayed, Shapiro laughed. 'That's the cinema next-door,' he explained. 'It's a one-way mirror. Let me keep an eye on things.'

'Must be difficult to stop keeping an eye on 'em.'

'Oh, you get used to it. I can pull the blind down if you like.'

Harry wondered whether he did – the two women were caressing one another with increasing enthusiasm – then decided it might be best if he concentrated on one thing at a time. 'I think it might help,' he admitted.

Shapiro laughed, handed Harry his drink, then lowered a blind that shut off the view just as one woman was gently nibbling at the breasts of the other.

'So. What've you got to tell me?'

'We've found him,' said Harry, wrenching his attention back to the matter in hand.

'Great.'

'He's living in Slough.'

'Oh, you are going to tell me that much, then.'

'I can tell you everything. Since he says he doesn't mind you knowing.'

''Course he doesn't,' said Shapiro, as though he'd proved his point. 'Why should he? I'm offering him a job and a holiday.

That has to be good news, especially the way Eric's fixed.'

'And what way's that?' enquired Harry, his curiosity awakening.

But Shapiro had his own brand of confidentiality. 'Oh, he's just had a rough time, that's all,' he said evasively. 'And that wife of his will make it even rougher if she can. He was keen on the idea of the holiday, was he?'

Harry nodded. 'Especially if it's somewhere abroad. Away from this lousy weather.'

'Oh, it'll be abroad all right. He needn't worry about that. I daresay he'll want it somewhere away from his lousy wife as well. So is he going to ring me or what?'

'I said you'd ring him,' said Harry, and he gave Shapiro the page of note-paper on which he'd written the number.

'Sure,' said Shapiro. 'I'll ring him tonight. And thanks, Harry boy, you've done a good job.'

'He didn't take a lot of finding.'

'It still needed doing. And you did it.'

He seemed in a talkative mood and wanting company. They compared notes on various mutual acquaintances, where they'd landed up, who were the successes and who the failures. Shapiro, it transpired, had a theory to explain the difference: why one man stayed in control of his life while another threw it away on drugs or booze or gambling.

'What you've got to have is family. Somebody to work for. Otherwise you've got nothing to lose and so you don't mind losing. Look at me. Married fifteen years. Three kids. Boy and two girls.' He waved a hand at the wall, and Harry saw, next to the one-way mirror which now had the blind over it, a photograph of three young Shapiros with three identical smiles.

'Very nice.'

'They're my life. They're what all this is about.' He made an expansive gesture that took in the sleazy club, the porno cinema and, by extension, all his other rat-infested properties. 'Everything I do is for them. Which is why it has to be good.' Then suddenly: 'What about yourself Harry? Are you married?'

'No,' admitted Harry.

'Regular lady-friend?'

'Oh. Yes.'

'But no kids.'

'No.'

'Well, that's what you need, Harry. Take it from me. Everybody should have at least three.'

Harry nodded and managed a quick glance at his watch. Mention of his lady-friend had reminded him it was getting late. But Shapiro had a new idea.

'I'll tell you what, Harry.'

'What?'

'You've done a good job for me, now I'd like to do a favour for you. Oh, I'll be paying you, don't worry. I mean a favour as a mark of our friendship.'

'Oh well . . . ' Harry muttered, not sure where this was leading.

'I have a villa in Spain. All mod cons. Very nice. You'd like it. Your lady, she'd definitely like it. Now why don't you borrow it? Have yourself a holiday. Get some of that sunshine you were talking about.'

'It's good of you but . . . ' Harry began.

'I mean it. Look.' He opened a drawer in his desk, fished around and produced a key-ring on which were three keys. 'There's the keys. Take 'em now if you like.'

'I only wish I could.'

'So why don't you?'

Why? Well, there was the Agency for one. For another, you didn't just pick up the keys to somebody's villa and walk out, even if it were somebody you knew well. Which in this case it wasn't. Not really.

'You need a rest, Harry. I can tell by looking at you.'

Perhaps he did. Yes. He'd been working a lot recently.

'And some sunshine. You need some sunshine.'

Oh well, certainly. Who didn't?

'Think about it. You know where I am. Give me a ring by the end of the week and let me know when you want to go.'

2.

Fisher's School in Westminster was an independent establishment catering for girls between the ages of eleven and eighteen. Its staff celebrated the end of each term with a sherry party on the evening of the final day.

'You don't really want me there,' Harry had objected when Jill reminded him of the one coming up before Easter.

They might have been living together in a basement flat in Islington but they each gave a wide berth to the career of the other. Harry's East End upbringing had made him wary of schools; Jill could never shake off her misgivings about the dubious world of private detection and the company it meant Harry keeping.

'I don't want to be there myself,' she retorted. 'If I have to go, I don't see why you shouldn't.'

'You teach there.'

'They want to see you,' she said, changing tack. 'They've heard me mention you and they're going to think there's something odd about you if you don't ever show your face.'

'There is something odd about me. A roomful of teachers scares me to death.'

'I'm a teacher. I don't scare you, do I?'

'Yes.'

'Oh, if you're just going to be stupid about it . . . !'

'Well, all right, you don't scare me, no. But I sleep with you, don't I?'

'So go ahead and sleep with all of them if you like. I just want you to bloody well be there for once.'

In the end, because it obviously mattered to her and because he was too tired to argue, he did as she wished, putting on a clean shirt and allowing her to drive him to the school, where he drank five glasses of medium dry sherry in the first half-hour.

13

They were gathered in the assembly-hall, an austere room that might once have seen happier days as a work-house. The walls were decorated with photographs of the entire school, year by year, and honours boards that recalled Head Girls and University Exhibitions and Scholarships. It reminded Harry of his own school, which had had its share of academic aspirations, enough anyway to expel him in his fifth year for lacing the staff-room tea with laxative.

'Right,' said Jill. 'Time you met somebody.'

'I'm quite happy standing here.'

'Come on,' she said, grasping him firmly by the elbow and leading him forward into the throng. 'Marcia, I want you to meet Harry. Harry, this is Marcia. She teaches Maths.'

'Pleased to meet you,' said Harry, stooping apologetically. Marcia was about four-ten and wore a sari.

Marcia said she was pleased to meet him too and turned to Jill. 'Is this the one who beat up your ex-hubby?'

'This is him,' said Jill.

'Good for you. The bastard needed it,' said Marcia. 'I must say she looks a lot happier since you came into her life. You're not planning on leaving her, are you?'

'Er, no,' said Harry.

'I hope not. You're better than a tonic for her.'

'Don't let her bully you,' said Jill. 'She bullies everybody.'

'I tell the truth,' said Marcia. 'And the truth is that you look at least ten years younger since you got involved with Harry here. Anyway, I'm going to circulate.' And then, as a parting shot to Harry: 'Are you enjoying this?'

'Of course he's not,' Jill answered for him. 'Does he look as though he's enjoying it?'

'No,' said Marcia. 'That's why I asked. But then nobody else is, so he needn't feel like he's the only one.'

'Thanks,' said Harry, managing his first smile of the evening.

Marcia went, and they stood silently together for a moment. Harry fingered his empty glass, and Jill gazed round, assessing where their next move should take them.

'I've booked us a holiday,' he said abruptly.

14

She stared at him in disbelief. 'You've what?'

'Booked us a holiday. Two weeks in Spain.'

'You are serious?'

'Oh yes.'

'And when is this holiday supposed to start?'

'Day after tomorrow.'

He'd intended to break it to her gently when they were alone together, but somehow the pressures of the sherry party had pushed him into blurting it out ahead of schedule. She looked at him in amazement.

'But why didn't you tell me? I mean I might not want to go to Spain.'

'Don't you?'

'I'm not saying I don't. Just that I might not have wanted to.'

'So do you?'

'I don't know,' she said, exasperated. 'I don't know what I want. I haven't had time to think about it.'

A stout, middle-aged woman in a blue-and-white dress bore down on them.

'Ah, Miss Handscombe,' she said. 'You're looking very nice this evening.'

'Thanks,' said Jill. 'So are you.'

'Oh well, I do what I can. But it's an up-hill struggle I'm afraid.'

'This is Harry,' said Jill. 'Harry, this is Miss Glendenning, the Deputy Headmistress.'

'Hello, Harry, nice to meet you,' said Miss Glendenning, shaking his hand. 'Are you in education too?'

'Not exactly, no . . .'

'He's a private detective,' said Jill.

'Really. That sounds jolly interesting.'

'And he's just told me he wants to take me to Spain the day after tomorrow.'

'My word.' Miss Glendenning looked at Harry with admiration. 'You don't let the grass grow under your feet, do you?'

'There were only two seats left on the flight,' explained Harry. 'If I wanted them I had to take them there and then.'

15

'And so you grabbed them while the going was good. And quite right too.'

'He might have asked me first,' muttered Jill.

'Why? He knew you'd only say yes. Well done, Harry. And if she doesn't want to go with you, then give me a shout and I'll go in her place.'

Harry laughed, liking Miss Glendenning and grateful for her support when Jill was still looking peevish. He knew she'd object to being taken for granted, not being fully consulted as befitted an equal member of their partnership. But he'd acted on impulse, saying yes to Leo Shapiro over his offer of the villa and then grabbing the air tickets while they were going.

'Well, have a super time,' said Miss Glendenning, and she launched herself at the next couple.

'Do you want to go or not?' Harry asked Jill quietly.

'Never mind do I want to go,' she countered. 'Why did it all have to be such a big secret?'

He knew suddenly that she was going to say yes and they would go. But she felt she owed it to herself to give him a hard time first.

'I had the offer of a villa,' he said patiently. 'A friend of mine . . . well, anyway, somebody I'd done some work for . . . he offered the loan of this villa. Then I checked on the flights, and it just seemed too good an opportunity to miss.'

'Whereabouts in Spain?'

'Costa del Sol.'

'What sort of a villa?'

'Well, I don't know. I mean I haven't seen a picture or anything. But he says it's very nice. All mod cons. Detached. Own swimming-pool.'

She looked at him in surprise. 'And who is he, then, this friend?'

'You've never met him,' he said, evasive. 'He's, er . . . he's a businessman.'

'And he's letting us borrow his villa? Just like that?'

'Yes.'

'Not charging us anything?'

16

'No.'

'What kind of businessman is he?'

'A generous one.'

'He sounds it.'

They were interrupted by the arrival of another member of staff, this time with husband in tow. On introduction, she turned out to be the Head of Biology; he was a self-employed electrician. Both were fairly stoned on sherry. Perhaps everyone else was by this time. Conversations had become animated, and there'd already been an accident with a bottle that had spiked the highly polished floor with splinters of broken glass. Harry was beginning to enjoy himself and listened while the Head of Biology explained her views on sex education, which were basically that there should be plenty of it.

Spain wasn't mentioned again till they left, coming out into the cold night. Behind them the party was still in full swing, and someone had set off a fire-extinguisher.

'Is it always like that?' asked Harry, for whom the evening had been a revelation.

Jill shrugged. 'Everybody always ends up pissed, if that's what you mean. It's relief that the term's over and they're that bit nearer their pensions.'

She insisted on driving and then, when they were on their way, said suddenly, 'You haven't even got a passport.'

'Yes, I have.'

'Well, you hadn't. You told me you'd never been abroad before.'

'I got one yesterday.'

'Well, all right then, what about me? How do you know my passport hasn't expired?'

'Because I had a look to see.'

'A clever bugger, aren't you?'

Harry smiled and said nothing. They drove along in silence, and he thought that's it, we're going. What's more, it hadn't been as painful as he'd expected. Compared to some of her protracted bouts of moodiness, this had been near to instant capitulation. Though not quite. Not yet.

17

'What about the Agency?' she said, finding a final obstacle to place in his path.

'We were going to close for a week anyway. Yvonne'll manage the second week by herself.'

And only when they were in bed and had made love did she at last say, 'OK.'

'You'll go . . . ?'

'Only because I know that if I don't you'll take Caroline Glendenning instead.'

They flew from Heathrow late in the afternoon. It was raining steadily, with the forecast offering little prospect of improvement. The airport's usual crowds were swollen by the extra holiday traffic. Harry had visited Heathrow before but never as a would-be passenger, and so the whole procedure of checking in and becoming part of that huge, continuous exodus had a novelty value for him that Jill found hard to share.

'I hate this place,' she said. 'It's like a mad-house. You actually feel that anybody at any time could go berserk and start shooting people.'

Harry looked around. Certainly a few people seemed on edge, their eyes never straying far from the departure boards, but for the most part they seemed to him an ordinary enough cross-section of non-lunatics, probably better-heeled than most to be able to afford the tickets in the first place. Yet Jill wasn't joking. He sensed a real tension in her, which only grew as their wait extended.

'Do you want a drink?' he offered.

'No.'

'Or something to eat? You hardly had any lunch.'

'If I eat anything I'll only throw up.'

'Oh, come on,' he said, surprised by her nervousness and hoping to jolly her back into a happier frame of mind. 'I thought you were supposed to be the experienced traveller.' For she'd told him of her trips that had taken in most of the countries of Europe and North Africa.

'That doesn't make any difference. I've always hated this bit.'

Two policemen went past, one of them clutching a sub-machine gun.

'Christ,' said Jill quietly.

'Oh well, I'm going to have a drink,' he said. 'You suit yourself.'

In the end she joined him and quickly downed two large brandies. Though, rather than cheering her up, these only made her annoyed with herself.

'Why do I get like this? I know that it's safer than travelling by car. It's ridiculous.'

'It is,' he agreed. 'Have another drink.'

'No. Though I wouldn't mind a cigarette.'

'You don't smoke,' he said in surprise.

'I used to. I feel like starting again.'

She bought a packet of Benson and Hedges and puffed away self-consciously till their flight was called. They filed on to a Boeing 737. Harry offered her the seat by the window.

'You take it,' she said. 'I don't want to see what's going on.'

A recorded announcement instructed them in the use of life-jackets and the position of the emergency exits, while a stewardess dutifully demonstrated. Harry listened with interest as around him more seasoned travellers read their newspapers. Jill sat staring ahead and seemed to be praying, though he knew her to be a fervent atheist.

They took off. Below them, London shrank and congealed and then disappeared completely as they rose through the clouds. Forget the Agency, thought Harry; for the next two weeks forget everything. Even Jill had relaxed, as though her terrors had remained earth-bound behind her.

'Sorry,' she said, patting his hand. 'I'm always like this. I'll be all right now.'

'Terrific.' A stewardess arrived with the drinks trolley. 'What do you want?'

'I think I could manage another brandy.'

After the drinks came a meal, served in a plastic container of many compartments with tiny packets of salt and pepper and a scented serviette. Harry consumed his, and most of Jill's, with

19

relish, then fell into a light sleep from which he was awakened by the plane beginning to circle and dip. Below them he glimpsed the packed suburbs of a city and a tangle of major roads, and then they were landing. Jill was concentrating hard on the flight magazine. They returned to earth with a bump and a shudder. People at once began to talk animatedly. Jill put away her magazine.

'Made it, then,' said Harry, gently teasing. 'What a surprise.'

She managed a smile. 'I always find it a surprise. Every time.'

They went out past a smiling stewardess and climbed stiffly down the steps to the tarmac. Though dusk was falling, the air was still sticky and warm. They were in Spain.

Leo's generosity had stretched to the laying on of a hire car at the airport. All Harry had to do was find it – not easy given the rows of identical Seats waiting for collection – then remember to drive on the right. They left Malaga airport following the signs that promised Marbella and Cadiz. Leo's villa was between Marbella and Fuengirola.

To their left was the sea and a thin strip of beach; the hills to their right were dotted with squat, white villas surrounded by trim gardens. Then, down closer to the roadside, there'd be the odd shop or garage, scruffy and with a corrugated roof.

It was wonderfully, blessedly warm. Though the sun had gone down, its heat still lingered. England, with its drizzle and cold winds, was now difficult to imagine. They passed Torre-molinos with its maze of hotels and then Marbella where children were playing in an illuminated park.

'So what do you think?' asked Jill, after being quiet for so long he thought she'd fallen asleep beside him.

'About what?'

'Spain.'

'There aren't as many bull-fighters as I'd expected.'

'It's their day off. Same for flamenco guitarists. Where are those directions?'

Harry managed to extract the paper Leo had given him from his back pocket while still driving with one hand.

'What lousy hand-writing,' said Jill, studying it. 'By the way, you have got the keys to the villa, haven't you?'

'Definitely.'

'You've about another five miles and then we have to look for a café called Ricco's.'

'We've just passed it,' said Harry.

'We can't have.'

'A sort of restaurant place with people sitting outside . . . ?'

'I don't know what it looks like. It just says here turn right at Café Ricco.'

'Well, that's what it was called. Ricco's.'

'Must be another one. How many miles have we done from the airport?'

He squinted at the dashboard. 'About seventy-five.'

'That's kilometres.' She looked at the paper again, working things out. 'Oh, shit. We'd better go back.'

'That was Ricco's . . . ?'

'Probably.'

They returned to it. It was a small bar-restaurant, garishly lit and with tables outside. There was the sound of pop music and the smell of food as they left the main highway and took the smaller road beside it. Here there were no lights.

'Slow down,' urged Jill. 'What did that sign say?'

'What sign?'

They had to reverse to find it. 'Calle Languza', it read.

'That's it,' said Jill, consulting her piece of paper. 'Now we want number forty-six.'

'Which way's that? Up or down?'

'I think we've already passed it.'

'Why not?' agreed Harry. 'We seem to be passing everything else tonight.'

He reversed slowly. They could now see that behind the hedges and wrought-iron gates lining the road were the pale outlines of villas and houses. Somewhere close a dog began to bark.

'Fifty-two,' said Jill, reading from a gate-post. 'Keep going.' And finally they were there. 'Forty-six. This is it.'

21

They got out of the car. Harry produced the keys Leo had given him, then became conscious of an unfamiliar sing-song noise that seemed to be all around them.

'What's that?' he asked Jill.

'Crickets. You'll get used to it.'

He found the key that unlocked the gate and they went through, stepping cautiously up a short pathway to the front door, which was of wood studded with iron. The lock here was of a sophisticated, high-security design. Typical of Leo Shapiro, Harry thought, but he said nothing.

Switching on the lights, they found themselves in an entrance hall that had a marble floor and white walls. The rooms going off it were furnished all to the same style, light and modern. There were glass-topped tables, boldly patterned cushions and abstract prints on the walls.

'Oh, very swish,' exclaimed Jill. To his relief, Harry saw she was pleased.

They went about, exploring, admitting to each other that the villa was larger and more luxurious than they'd expected. The windows of the lounge opened on to a terrace, beyond which was an extensive garden. A grille of wrought ironwork denied access till Harry used his third key to open it.

And there was their swimming-pool, still and dark. Harry stooped and tested the water with his hand.

'What's it like?' asked Jill, coming out behind him.

'Cold.'

She laughed. 'They always are.' Then she yawned and stretched. 'Though I must admit, Harry Sommers, this isn't at all bad. I reckon I can put up with it quite happily for the next two weeks.'

'It's bloody marvellous,' he said. 'Come on, be honest. It's . . . well, it's perfect.'

'It is. And thanks. I'm sorry I was such a pain about coming here.'

'You weren't. Well, no more than usual.'

He took her in his arms and they kissed, breaking apart when what he took to be two small birds came circling wildly about their heads. Jill laughed and pointed out they were bats, not birds, and he saw she was right.

They busied themselves with bringing in the luggage and unpacking. Jill reconnoitred the kitchen and offered him a choice of omelette or scrambled eggs. He chose the omelette, then asked her what she'd like to drink.

'What is there?'

'Everything.' He, too, had been searching around and had come upon a drinks cabinet stuffed with bottles.

'Do you think we should take his booze, though?' Jill asked, scrupulous as ever.

'I'm sure we should. He won't even notice.'

Later she drew his attention to a row of framed photographs that stood in one of the bedrooms. They were of Leo Shapiro and his family, the three children whose picture Harry had already seen at the club and a woman he took to be their mother. One had been taken beside the swimming-pool, the smiling faces squinting against the sunlight. Another was of the children on the beach, while a third was of his wife standing alone and looking self-conscious in her bikini.

'That's your friend, is it?' said Jill, pointing to Shapiro.

'Yes,' admitted Harry reluctantly.

'So who're these people, then, do you know?' she asked, picking up another photograph. It showed Shapiro again, but this time he was seated at a table with four other men, all of them smiling and raising glasses towards the camera.

'No idea.'

She peered more closely. 'That's the café where we turned, isn't it?'

The sign 'Café Ricco' appeared in a corner of the picture.

'I suppose it must be.'

She sensed his evasiveness. 'Do you know them?'

'No.' Which was true but didn't satisfy her.

'Harry, exactly what line of business is he in, this friend of yours?'

'Oh, one thing and another.'

She sighed. 'That means you don't want to tell me. Which

means it's either illegal or nasty or both.'

'Look, does it matter?' he protested. 'He's just somebody who's lent us this place. I mean he's not going to be here. You're never going to meet him.'

'And what about his friends?'

'What about them?'

'They might be here, mightn't they?'

He hesitated, not wanting to admit that the possibility had already occurred to him. 'They could be anybody,' he said. 'Just people who were here on holiday. Anybody.'

'So then why has he framed their photograph and stuck it in his bedroom?' she asked with her usual relentless logic.

'I've no idea. Look, what does it matter anyway?'

He knew of course. But was hoping she wouldn't and would let the matter drop.

'They might be criminals,' she said, and he knew his hopes were in vain. 'They might be living over here to escape prosecution in England.'

'That's ridiculous.'

'Why is it? People do it. I've read about them.'

'Yes, but . . . Look, you've seen a photograph of a bunch of men neither of us knows and you're jumping to all sorts of crazy conclusions. And even if you're right, so what? We don't have to meet them.'

She looked at him in a way that always made him feel she could read his mind. 'I hope not.'

'For Christ's sake . . . !'

'I hope not, Harry. I really do.'

She left the matter there, announcing she needed a bath and disappearing. He helped himself to a scotch and had another, closer look at the photograph. They were all men in their late thirties or early forties, evidently having a good time, but more than that you couldn't tell. They might have been bank managers. Well, no, probably not bank managers, but it was surely stretching things to label them as criminals on such slight acquaintance.

He went outside and locked the front gate. He saw now that

its iron bars were continued inside the hedging that bordered the property so that everything, villa and gardens, was enclosed in a rectangular cage. There was also a criss-cross of iron bars over each of the windows.

The bats were still cavorting above the dark swimming-pool, and the crickets keeping up their thin wail.

3.

The sun was up before they were. Harry left Jill sleeping, pulled on a pair of shorts and wandered from the bedroom, taking a moment to get his bearings. The villa, impressive enough on last night's first encounter, appeared now even more luxurious, its rooms spacious and cool. Harry unlocked the gates that enclosed the patio and went out to where the pool was now bright with sunlight and the paving around it hot to his feet.

He hesitated a moment, steadied himself, then took a shallow dive, enjoying the shock of the water. A few strokes brought him to the far end; then, as he kicked off to return, he caught a glimpse of Jill watching from the doorway.

'Come on in,' he called.

'Later.'

'Now,' he insisted. 'It's marvellous.' And, to illustrate, he powered himself the length of the pool, spreading a wake behind him that slapped up against the sides.

'I'm hungry now,' she said, resisting. 'I can't swim on an empty stomach.' And she disappeared back into the relative darkness of the villa.

Harry, swimming up and down the pool, wondered briefly about the prospects for late-night swims under a full moon, naked and with no-one to interrupt them. Wasn't that one of the main attractions of having a pool of your very own? After another ten short lengths, he heaved himself out and stood dripping and slightly breathless. With time now to notice, he saw the garden was thick with bushes and vivid flowers, some familiar though he didn't know their names, others strange and exotic.

Jill was in the kitchen, making coffee. She was wearing a white shirt that came down to her thighs. He put his arms around her waist and nuzzled into her neck.

'You're wet.' She flinched away.

'Sorry,' he said, stepping back.

'And you're dripping all over the floor.'

'Sorry, sorry, sorry,' he sang out, retreating further to the doorway. He could see the idea of nude swimming would have to be broached with care.

'Now,' she said, standing before the open refrigerator, 'you can have anything you want for breakfast. So long as it's eggs.'

'Oh well, I'll have eggs, then.'

'And then I think we'd better do some shopping. How are we off for pesetas?'

'About twenty quid's worth. The rest's in traveller's cheques.'

'So we'd better find a bank.'

They had breakfast – boiled eggs and coffee – outside in the garden. Jill threw off her shirt to reveal a skimpy turquoise bikini.

'Very nice,' said Harry.

'Thanks. But if we're not careful we're both going to end up looking like over-ripe tomatoes. Since you thought of everything else, did you think of suntan oil?'

'No,' he admitted.

'Then it's a good thing I did.' She marched back indoors and returned with a tube of something and, more surprisingly, with the packet of cigarettes she'd bought at Heathrow.

'Oh, I see,' said Harry.

'What?' She extracted one and placed it between her lips, then removed it again to say, 'It's all right, I can do it,' as he reached for the matches to light it for her.

'I didn't think you meant it when you said you were starting smoking again.'

'It's only while we're here. I'll stop when we get back.'

'I'll get you an ashtray.'

He found one in the bedroom, beside the photograph of Shapiro and his cronies that had so alarmed and antagonised Jill the night before. Lest it might do so again, he moved it so it was more or less hidden behind the more innocent pictures of

27

Shapiro's skinny missus and his photo-fit kids.

He returned with the ashtray. They sat and had another cup of coffee, sharing a reluctance to venture out and, anyway, conscious of the leisurely two weeks stretching before them. It was a novelty, this feeling of time to spare, time to waste. Till they heard a bell ringing back inside the villa and looked at one another in surprise.

'What's that?' asked Jill.

'Alarm clock?' suggested Harry.

'Hardly. I didn't touch anything. Did you?'

'No.'

They were both half-turned, waiting for something further; then, when it didn't come, sank back again on to their reclining chairs.

'Might have been the telephone,' offered Harry.

'I don't think telephones sound like that,' she said, stifling a yawn, 'even in Spain.'

The bell rang again, this time with a long, more urgent ringing that brought both their heads round and Harry to his feet.

'It's the door-bell,' said Jill.

'Can't be. The front gate's still locked.'

'Well, is there a bell on the gate, then?'

'I'll go and see.' He remembered something Shapiro had mentioned and called back to her as he left: 'It's probably the maid. There's supposed to be a maid comes in to clean up.'

'She'd have her own key,' said Jill.

He didn't stay to dispute that but trotted round the side of the villa and saw immediately a flash of movement through the wrought ironwork of the gate. 'Coming,' he called and saw it was a woman, possibly in her twenties, certainly good-looking. She had a mane of platinum blonde hair to shoulder length and was wearing jeans and a tee-shirt that said 'Hertz Rent-A-Car'.

'I hope I haven't got you up,' she said, with a broad smile that suggested she knew he'd forgive her if she had.

'You haven't, no,' he reassured her as he struggled to unlock the gate.

28

'Well, I'm glad about that. Only I thought I'd better catch you before you set off for the beach or somewhere.'

He swung open the gate. 'Come in.'

She did, holding out a hand tipped with bright red nails. 'I'm Rebecca Connors. And you're Harry, yes?'

'Yes.'

Without the bars of the gate between them, she was revealed as very lovely indeed, with a golden tan, statuesque figure, hazel eyes. And toenails painted to match her fingers.

'Leo phoned and said you'd be coming. Asked me if I'd call and say hiya. So here I am.'

'Nice of him,' said Harry. 'I mean nice of you. We thought you must be the maid.'

She raised an eyebrow. 'I don't do my own dusting, never mind anybody else's.'

'No,' he said, feeling stupid. 'I can see . . . I mean as soon as I saw you . . . '

'I don't look like a maid? So what do I look like?'

Rather than answer that, he said, 'Why don't you come round? We're in the garden.'

'OK, but I can't stop for long. Duty calls and all that. And how was your flight? You obviously got here, so nothing very terrible happened.'

'Yes. I mean no, it didn't.'

They came round to where Jill was waiting. She'd put the white shirt back on, hiding her bikini.

'Er, Jill, this is . . . '

'Rebecca Connors. Hello.' And she shook Jill's hand.

'Hello,' said Jill, returning the smile, though guardedly, already on the defensive.

'Sit down,' Harry said. 'Would you like a coffee?'

'No, I won't,' she said, perching on the edge of the chair he dragged forward. 'I'm supposed to be opening up the office.' She indicated her breasts, or at least the lettering across them.

'Rebecca's a . . . a friend of Leo's,' said Harry. 'The man who's lent us the villa.'

'That Leo,' said Jill.

29

'And you two are from London?' Rebecca asked.

'Yes,' said Harry.

'Me too. Though it's about ten years since I last set eyes on it. I can't stand England any more. Everybody's so bloody tight-arsed.'

'Really,' said Jill.

'There's no sun, the food's lousy and they get screwed up about sex.'

'Perhaps you were just unlucky in the people you knew,' said Jill.

Harry stepped in quickly. 'So you've been over here a fair while?'

'A couple of years. Before that I was in the States and before that one place and another.'

'Great,' he said, stuck for a response.

She shrugged. 'Well, it means my sins have further to go to catch up with me. And I'm not the only one round here. There's quite a crowd of us. All ex-pat Brits sticking together. So Leo thought it'd be nice if I said hello and then introduced you to a few people.'

'That'd be very kind of you,' said Harry, and he prompted Jill: 'Wouldn't it?'

'Yes,' she said.

'Do either of you speak Spanish?' asked Rebecca.

'Not a word,' said Harry.

'No,' said Jill, who'd earlier told him she'd passed O-level when at school. 'Do you?'

'Enough. But what the hell, you hardly need it round here. Just let me know if you have any problems.'

'You live locally?' asked Harry.

'Well, I've this tiny flat in Marbella. About the size of a cupboard. But it's somewhere to keep a spare pair of knickers.' Then, abruptly: 'Leo says you're some kind of detective?'

Harry shrugged. 'The private kind.'

Rebecca turned to Jill. 'You work with him?'

'No.'

Feeling that more was called for, Harry added, 'Jill's a teacher.'

'Yes? I've a sister who's a teacher. She hates it. Says the kids are bastards and the staff are worse. Do you hate it?'

'Not at the moment,' said Jill evenly as she lit another cigarette.

'Mind, my sister's a bitch. If I had kids I wouldn't want her near them.' She looked at her watch. 'Christ, is that the time? I've got to go. But first – why I wanted to catch you now – there's a few of us getting together tonight and I wondered if you'd like to join us.'

'We hadn't really made any plans yet, had we?' Jill said firmly, looking at Harry.

'No, but . . . well . . . '

'Oh, it's no big deal,' said Rebecca. 'In fact, it happens most nights. Did you notice the café where you turned off the main road?'

'Café Ricco,' said Jill.

'Yes, well, we tend to hang out there. Mainly because it's convenient. And Alan – that's one of the gang – he's screwing one of the waiters.'

'That is convenient,' said Jill.

'And I'm sort of semi-shacked up with Norris, who's . . . well, you'll meet him if you come along. He has a villa just up the road from here, so I tend to be in the vicinity when I'm not hiding in my tiny cupboard. So we're going to be there anyway. Why don't you just drop in if you feel like it?'

'We will,' said Harry. 'It's good of you to ask us.'

'OK. So we'll be seeing you,' she said, and stood up.

'What time?' asked Harry, also standing. Jill hadn't moved.

'Oh, we'll be there some time between eight and nine. Well, it's been great meeting you both. I hope you're going to have a good holiday.'

'Thanks,' said Harry.

'I'll see myself out. *Ciao*.' And, with a final smile that took in both of them, she strode away, disappearing round the side of the villa.

There was a silence after she'd gone. Harry cleared his

31

throat, then sat down. 'Well,' he said.

Jill stubbed out her cigarette, gathered up the suntan lotion and inserted her toes back into the slip-ons she'd kicked off. 'I suppose we'd better do that shopping,' she said. 'Before we have any more visitors.'

The question of whether they'd join Rebecca's little get-together that evening was raised by neither till they'd toured the shelves of the local *supermercardo* and loaded a trolley with basics for their stay. They avoided the meat counter but went instead for the fish, which was there in abundance. 'Not surprising,' said Jill, 'considering where we are.' They chose sword-fish steaks, *calamares* ('squid', she explained) and a parcel of *gambas* ('prawns – only bigger'). Wine was also in abundance, and they piled the trolley with bottles of Rioja.

'We can always leave it if we don't drink it all,' she said.

'Oh, we'll drink it,' said Harry.

'Well, we might. But not if you're out drinking with your new-found friends every night.'

So, as they came to the check-out, they also came to the topic he knew had to be aired sooner or later.

'What new-found friends?' he asked patiently.

'Rebecca and her gang,' said Jill, as the young girl on the till whipped through their purchases at lightning speed.

'Come on,' he urged gently. 'They're only trying to be friendly.'

'But who are they, Harry?'

'I don't know. Friends of Shapiro's.'

'The men in the photograph.'

'Could be. But so what? They've only invited us for a drink. We don't have to go if we don't want to.'

The girl on the till pointed to a total, and Jill concentrated on sorting out the wad of notes they'd collected earlier from the Banco de Madrid. Harry picked up the three brown bags into which their purchases had been piled and led the way out to the car.

'You want us to go, though, don't you?' Jill said, following.

'Well, why not? It'll look peculiar if we don't.' Then, before driving off, he repeated, 'But, like I say, it's up to you. If you don't want to go, then we won't.'

'I don't know,' she said. 'Let me think about it.'

'Sure.'

That afternoon they went down to the beach, which turned out to be a relatively quiet stretch featuring a ramshackle restaurant and a bearded young man who made elaborate religious sculptures from sand. There were single people reading paperback novels, a group of youngsters playing tapes and families with children. Harry and Jill lay on their towels and rubbed oil on to one another's backs.

'I am being tight-arsed, aren't I?' said Jill suddenly.

'What?'

'About meeting these people tonight. I'm being exactly like she said. And I mean why? Of course we must go.'

He knew she was making an effort for his sake but thought, well, why shouldn't she for once?

'Good,' he said. 'We can always leave if you don't like it.'

'Of course I'll like it. I'm determined to like it.'

He laughed. 'I love you.'

'Then prove it. Go and buy me a coke or anyway something cold.'

'Will do.'

He lifted himself off his towel and trod across the hot sand towards the ramshackle restaurant and past the sand-sculptor who was completing a gigantic crucifix.

'Terrific,' said Harry in appreciation.

'*Danke*,' said the sand-sculptor, evidently German.

The thought occurred to him that Jill's hackles had risen at Rebecca's first appearance, before she'd even mentioned the invitation. How far had it mattered that she'd been anything but an anonymous messenger but in fact an extremely sexy blonde who'd made them both feel like the tourists they were with their suntan oil and mottled English complexions? Was it Rebecca herself she'd been wary of as much as Shapiro's cronies?

He successfully collected two cokes, paid for them and

33

carried them back across the beach to where she was lying.

'Look,' she said.

'Where?'

'Coming out of the sea.'

As she spoke, the waves ebbed to reveal two men in frogman gear plodding doggedly through the surf towards them. One carried a harpoon-gun. Both were dragging something behind them. As they advanced and rose from the water, Harry saw it was a net in which something writhed.

'What have they got?' asked Jill, her eyes wide.

Harry shook his head. 'Some kind of fish, is it?'

The frogmen advanced on to the sands. Behind them their net drained of water and showed that it contained an eel, a coiled, muscular conger eel that must have been all of five or six feet long.

'It's still alive,' said Jill fearfully.

They cautiously tipped it from the net, then stood looking at it as it writhed on the sand. Finally one of them unsheathed his knife and circled behind it, waited till it settled for a moment, then stabbed hard and without hesitation into the area just behind its head. The eel straightened like a cracked whip, then flung itself from side to side in a paroxysm of protest.

The other frogman said something which made his colleague laugh. Then, choosing his moment, he bent and withdrew the knife, then struck again. This time there was the sound of gristle and bone giving way. The eel kicked again but with less force. The two frogmen stood, hands on hips, now content to wait as the eel's movements slowed and stopped. Then one of them extracted the knife and stuck it back, experimentally, into the conger's neck. There was no response.

They unstrapped their flippers, then one of them slung the inert conger over his shoulder and they set off together up the beach.

Harry had a shower, got dressed and tried watching Spanish television while Jill applied her make-up and waited for her hair to dry. The television offered a choice between news and drama, both equally unintelligible. He switched it off and went for a walk round the garden.

'Ready, then?'

She came out to join him in a pale green-and-white dress he hadn't seen before that made her look younger, almost girlish.

'You've caught the sun,' he said, taking her hand.

She laughed. 'Be difficult not to. Anyway, you should talk. You look as though you've been here a month at least.'

Seeing it was barely eight o'clock and not wanting to be early, they decided on a drink before setting out and opened one of the bottles of wine bought that morning.

'Here's to us,' said Harry.

'To us.'

'You know, I could very easily get used to this,' he said, meaning the villa and the life of leisure that went with it.

'Then it's probably a good thing you can't afford it.'

'I wonder how much these places cost. I mean I know I can't afford it. I just wonder who can.'

They speculated about how much Shapiro must have invested to allow them their holiday and decided they were best not knowing and certainly not having to pay it.

'Shall we go?' suggested Harry, as the crickets had started their sing-song and the sun was beginning to set.

'Why not?'

She dropped the remaining cigarettes into her handbag – 'Just in case I decide I want one. It doesn't mean I'm going to smoke my head off.' Harry took the keys and did the rounds of locking up. The road outside was deserted save for a few parked cars. Their own car they decided to leave, as the Café Ricco was no more than a few minutes' walk away.

'Anyway, we don't want you getting breathalysed,' said Jill.

'Do they have them here?'

'Probably. Best not find out.'

It struck Harry that the most surprising thing about being abroad was how much of it was familiar. Coca-Cola, Volvos, the brands of washing-powders . . . and now breathalysers. The world was smaller than he'd imagined.

They ambled hand in hand down the road towards the café, whose coloured lights were already in view. There were no real pavements, and cars were parked tight against the hedges, forcing them into single file as they passed.

'There's your friend,' said Jill.

'My friend . . . ?'

'Rebecca what's-her-name.'

Conspicuous with her shock of blonde hair, she was at an outside table with a group of four or five other people. Whether these were the men who appeared in the photograph with Shapiro it was impossible yet to say. Rebecca, however, must have been watching for them and now raised a hand in greeting. Harry gave a wave back.

'She's very attractive,' said Jill.

'Yes, well . . . so are you.'

'Thanks,' she said, and gave a little laugh.

They moved out into the road to pass a parked Mercedes. 'Careful,' warned Harry, hearing a motor approaching from behind. They stopped to let it go by, not a car but a light motorcycle carrying two young men. No helmets, registered Harry. At least that regulation hadn't been exported.

The bike slowed as it came to them. The pillion-rider leant out and grabbed the handbag Jill was holding in her hand. She clutched at it instinctively but too late. The bike was away and the bag with it.

Too late also was Harry's reaction. He'd watched open-mouthed and disbelieving as it had happened and now could only call, 'Hey . . . !' and sprint forward in a futile gesture of pursuit. Jill, too, found her voice. 'My bag!' she cried, and began to run after him, though awkwardly in her high heels.

Then, as the bike reached the café, a chair was flung beneath it. It skidded across the road and hit the hedge on the other side, already minus its two riders, who'd gone sprawling. The men with Rebecca, one of whom had flung the chair, were on their feet and reached the young thieves before either could escape. Without delay, they set into them, kicking the one still down and landing blows on the other who'd managed to

36

scramble to his feet.

Harry arrived at a run and then Jill behind him. Her handbag lay ignored in the road. Other customers were hurrying out from the café. The motorcyclist on the ground was unconscious, the other yelling with pain and fear at the battering he was still receiving.

4.

There was a general call for restraint, Spanish and English voices competing to be heard, before the beating stopped. Harry, for once, felt like a by-stander, unsure of what to do next and grateful for Rebecca's presence. Presumably it was she who'd alerted her friends to the theft and spurred them into action. She was now trying to calm things, helped by the burly, older man who was with her and who, when words failed, grabbed his over-enthusiastic colleague, still aiming blows at the cowering Spanish youth, and roughly pushed him back into the café.

Jill retrieved her handbag. Harry put an arm around her.

'Go and sit down,' Rebecca told them. 'We'll take care of it.'

The youth on the floor stirred and was sick.

'Shouldn't somebody see to him?' asked Jill, concerned. With the tables now turned, she was no longer the victim and had time to feel pity for those who were.

Rebecca harangued the other youth, evidently telling him to see to his wretched accomplice.

'Tell them to bugger off,' said the burly man. 'Before they get another dose.'

Nobody seemed interested in calling the police. Indeed, there were cries of alarm when a police-car cruised by on the main road but didn't stop. Eventually the two youths went limping away, leaving their damaged motorcycle behind. Harry hoisted it out of the way of any traffic, then went with Jill to join the party gradually reassembling around a table. Drinks were poured. There was a mood of celebration, as after a victory. The café's loudspeakers were playing the old Rolling Stones number 'I Can't Get No Satisfaction'.

'Just what I needed,' grinned the over-keen assailant, who was called Gerald Fieldhouse. 'Give me an appetite.'

'It's what they deserve,' sniffed his girl-friend beside him. 'They pinch anything. It's got so's you can't walk down the street.'

She was called Samantha but she asked Harry and Jill to call her Sam because everybody else did. She had curly black hair, a salmon-pink tan and a spoiled, pouting expression.

There was a general chorus of agreement that street crime was rife. Women didn't dare carry bags or wear jewellery any more, and it was wise to carry no more money than was essential. Gypsies, they said, were behind most of it, hawking their embroidered tablecloths around the resorts while on the look-out for richer pickings.

Norris Edgerton, Rebecca's boy-friend, added his voice. 'There are all these police about but they don't any of 'em do nothing. That's why you're better off sorting it out yourself.'

Rebecca gave Harry a sly smile which he interpreted as meaning this wasn't the whole story. Perhaps then Norris and friends had other, more compelling reasons for not wanting to involve the police. He glanced sideways at Jill to see how she was taking things. In fact, she seemed to be enjoying herself, talking animatedly to the other member of the group, who'd been introduced as Alan Mullins. He had the look of an ageing teddy-boy with his long, cultivated side-boards. Very East End. On first sight Harry had wondered whether he'd met him before somewhere but he couldn't think where it might have been, and Mullins had shown no sign of mutual recognition.

The faces of all three men were familiar to him from the photograph they'd come across in Shapiro's villa. No doubt about that. It had been these three plus Shapiro and one more who'd made up the convivial group.

More wine was sent for.

'Let me get this —' Harry started to say but was shouted down.

'You're a guest. You're both guests,' said Norris, who seemed to be group leader in so far as there was one. 'You're not paying. She' – indicating Jill – 'needn't have brought her handbag after all.'

There was general mirth at this, which even Jill shared. The brief encounter with violence didn't seem to have sickened her as Harry feared it might. Instead, Rebecca's dubious companions had emerged as allies, white knights charging to the rescue, even if Fieldhouse and Mullins had done so with undue relish. It had also prompted her to drink faster than usual, which probably wasn't a bad thing under the circumstances.

'Right, I'm starving,' said Norris. 'Are we eating here or going somewhere else?'

The consensus was for staying, and so menus were sent for and orders placed with the young Italian waiter, good-looking and elegantly coiffured, whom Harry guessed must be Mullins's boy-friend, the one Rebecca had referred to earlier.

'So how's old England, then?' said Norris once the food had been decided on.

'Oh, much as usual,' said Harry. 'Raining a lot.'

'You brought any English papers with you?'

Harry shook his head, and Rebecca said, 'You can buy them here, for Christ's sake.'

'Some of 'em. But you can't buy all of 'em, can you?'

'So? Who in their right mind wants to read every English newspaper? I sometimes wonder why you don't just move back there.'

'You must be joking. What about football, Harry? You follow anybody in particular?'

'West Ham.'

'Great team,' said Mullins. 'Used to follow them myself.'

'Well, I don't get down there much these days,' Harry admitted. 'Too much work.'

'This is as a private detective, right?' said Norris.

'Yes.'

Fieldhouse laughed. 'I've known a lot of detectives and they all like a bit of private work, given half a chance. You know what I mean?'

'We all know what you mean,' said Norris.

'A little drinks money. Something for the back pocket.'

'I once went out with a policeman,' said Sam, and giggled. 'Only I didn't know he was a policeman, not when I went out

40

with him. He said he was a security adviser or expert or something, I can't remember now.'

'Show you his truncheon, did he?' said Fieldhouse.

She tutted. 'I knew you were going to say that.'

'All right, so I've said it. So did he or didn't he?'

She ignored him and lit a cigarette with a gold lighter shaped like a dolphin.

'What is it you do, matrimonial work, stuff like that?' asked Norris.

Harry shrugged. 'All sorts. Some of it's matrimonial.'

'You don't still have to sneak in with a camera and catch 'em at it?' asked Rebecca.

'Not any more.'

'So you're all right,' said Fieldhouse with a grin. 'Nothing to worry about.'

It was a joke that didn't go down too well with Rebecca, who said, 'Fuck off, Gerald', and turned back to Harry. 'So what do you do if you don't take pictures of couples humping?'

'Oh, a lot of it's legal work. Process-serving, that kind of thing. Then we're sometimes asked to trace missing people, following husbands or wives to see what they're up to. Then there's industrial work, security work . . . but you'd generally go to a bigger firm for that.'

'And how does it pay, then?' asked Norris, interested. 'You make a bob or two?'

'That's about all. You're never going to get rich on it.'

'Haven't I seen you somewhere before?' said Mullins, who'd been eyeing Harry throughout this. 'I mean I get the impression we might have worked together somewhere.'

'Don't tell us you were once a private detective,' chortled Fieldhouse. 'That I won't believe.'

'No. I think it might have been in a club or somewhere like that.'

Harry admitted that he, too, thought they might have met before and reeled off a few names of the places he'd worked as barman or bouncer.

'That's it,' said Mullins when he mentioned 'Caroline's', a

club in Streatham that had been owned by a retired jockey and named after his daughter. 'Caroline's, yes. I'd forgotten all about that place. Must have been a good ten or twelve years ago, must that.'

'I was on the door,' said Harry.

'I was in the band. Bass guitar and vocals.'

'Give us a song, then,' said Fieldhouse.

'And what do you do now?' said Jill.

Mullins's hesitation was fractional; then he said, 'As little as possible. And for as short a time as possible.'

'It's more a question of what he'd find himself doing if he went back home,' said Fieldhouse.

'So you're a permanent resident here?' said Jill, seemingly determined on pursuing the matter.

Harry began to worry: was she going to turn difficult after all?

'I suppose I am, yes,' said Mullins. 'Till I move on somewhere else.'

'We're all permanent residents, love,' said Norris, taking over. 'We've all had our little disagreements with Her Majesty, you see. And I mean you hear about all this over-crowding in British prisons . . . well, us staying over here, it sort of helps 'em out. Means they're not adding to the numbers.'

He stated it calmly, as though to indicate Jill could either take it or leave it. To Harry's relief, she seemed inclined to accept the situation with none of her customary soul-searching. Perhaps the struggle over her handbag really had placed them all firmly on the same side. As well as the wine she was still happily consuming. All she said was, 'I see. So it's a sort of enforced exile.'

'That's about the top and bottom of it,' said Norris.

'A fucking marvellous exile,' said Fieldhouse. 'I mean look at what we've got here compared to England. I mean, given the chance, they'd all be here in fucking exile, all that have any sense.'

'I must admit I don't think I could ever get used to that cold weather again,' agreed Mullins.

'Me neither,' agreed Fieldhouse. 'I mean look at this place.

You've got the sun, you've got the, er . . . ' He ran out of inspiration. 'Well, you've got the fucking sun. What more could anybody want?'

'I go back home every now and again,' said Sam. 'Just for the odd week. See my family. They never seem to try and stop me or anything.'

'Who doesn't?' asked Fieldhouse.

'Well, anybody. The police or anybody.'

'So why should they? I mean what have you ever done?'

'Well no, but I mean I'm with you, aren't I? You'd think that'd be enough.'

'I bet they follow you. I bet there's somebody keeping an eye on you.'

'No, there isn't. 'Cause I'd see 'em if there was.'

'You wouldn't see 'em. You think you would but you wouldn't see 'em if they didn't want you to. Ask him. He's a detective. They could follow her and she wouldn't be any the wiser, would she?'

'No use asking me,' said Harry, preferring to sit this one out. 'They're the real professionals you're talking about now.'

'She wouldn't see 'em.'

''Course I fucking would.'

The food arrived, a mixed bag of pizzas and chicken and fish, with salad and chips. The Italian waiter sorted out which went to whom.

'You all right?' Mullins asked him.

'Very well, thank you,' he said formally, and smiled.

'Good.'

'And bring us two more bottles of this wine,' said Norris. '*Vino*. Two of 'em. *Pronto*.'

He wasn't, though, doing much drinking himself. Harry noticed how both he and Rebecca had switched to mineral water after their first glass or two. It was mainly Fieldhouse and his girl Sam who were putting the *vino* away, ably assisted by Mullins, Jill and Harry. He was conscious, too, of the way Rebecca hadn't played much part in the conversation but had sat back, keeping a quizzical eye on himself and Jill as though there was something about them she couldn't quite weigh up. More than once he'd intercepted her gaze, whereupon she'd given a quick smile and been happy to hold eye-contact till he'd been the first to look away again.

Fieldhouse poured himself some more wine. 'Tell you what, let's have a toast.' He raised his glass. 'Absent friends.'

'Absent friends,' echoed Jill, then looked surprised at hearing herself say it. She was the only one who'd responded.

'Anybody heard anything yet?' asked Fieldhouse. There was a silence. Norris and Mullins were concentrating on their meals. 'About Tommy? Any news or anything?'

'No,' said Norris shortly.

It struck Harry that Tommy – whoever he was – was a topic Norris would rather not have raised. Sam, though, either was less perceptive or didn't give a damn whether Norris wanted it raised or not.

'So what's going to happen, then?' she said. 'I mean there's his house, isn't there? And his car. That's still there because I saw it this morning.'

'No idea,' said Norris.

'Well, surely somebody ought to do something.'

'Somebody will.'

Rebecca laughed, seeing the puzzlement on Harry's face. 'It's a friend of ours, Tommy Smith. Another of the Costa del Sol exiles.'

'You don't have to tell everybody,' said Norris, disapproving.

'I'm not telling everybody. I'm telling Harry. All right?' From Norris's expression it didn't seem to be, but she continued anyway: 'Tommy was one of the gang. One of the regulars. In fact, he's been over here longer than anybody.'

'Longer than me, anyway,' said Mullins.

'Right, and then one day he just wasn't around any more. He'd disappeared. That was, what, about three or four weeks ago now.'

'Four weeks tomorrow,' said Sam.

'And we've been round to his villa, which is all locked up, but it looks like everything's there inside.'

44

'And his car,' said Sam. 'That's just stood outside the gate. Never been moved.'

'So nobody knows where he's got to. It's like the *Marie Celeste*. One of life's little mysteries.'

'Suppose he's still inside?' asked Jill, intrigued. 'I mean suppose something's happened to him? Perhaps he's been taken ill and he's still there inside his villa?'

'That's what I've said,' agreed Sam.

Norris came back to life. 'He's not inside. There's nobody inside.'

'Oh, and how would you know that?'

'Because I've been in and had a look. I went in when the maid was there. I got her to let me in and have a look around.'

'Well, why didn't you say?' Sam protested. Rebecca, too, looked at him in surprise as though this was also news to her.

Norris went on eating and said calmly, 'I'm saying now, aren't I? Everything's just as it should be. Like he decided to leave it and just take himself off somewhere. He's entitled. He doesn't have to make any announcements about it.'

'He was always a nutter, was Tommy,' said Fieldhouse.

'Has he taken his passport?' asked Jill.

Norris paused, then said, 'I don't know. I didn't see it but then I wasn't exactly pulling the place apart.'

'Wouldn't prove anything anyway,' said Mullins. 'Sometimes you travel better without a passport. Just depends where he was going.'

'Or whether he's thinking of coming back again,' said Fieldhouse.

'Yes, think about that,' said Norris. 'I mean, he wouldn't be too delighted if we made a song and dance and then he came walking back in and found the civil guard all over his living-room wanting to know where he'd been and what he'd been getting up to. Wouldn't be too delighted at all.'

They thought about it and nodded in agreement.

'I still think it's peculiar,' said Sam defiantly.

'Think all you want,' said Norris. 'Just be careful what you're saying.' It was an announcement that the topic was closed. 'So what about this diabolical government you've got, Harry? I mean, never mind the weather, when's that going to change?'

They talked about politics, then about TV programmes and comparative food prices. Jill asked about politics in post-Franco Spain, but they shied away from her questions, earnestly proclaiming their ignorance. As if, by ignoring the Spaniards, they'd encourage the Spaniards to ignore them.

'You get to see much football here?' Harry asked Mullins.

'I've been to the odd match but . . . well, it's not the same, is it?'

'You want to try the bull-fights,' enthused Fieldhouse. 'Fucking amazing.'

'You're not getting me there again,' said Sam with a shudder.

'No. Shan't be wanting to neither.' He turned to the others. 'She pesters me to take her, then when I do she wants to leave after the first bull.'

'I felt sick.'

'I said all right, you leave if you want to but I'm staying.'

'I had to go and sit by myself in the sodding car.'

'I need to find the ladies',' said Jill. 'Inside, is it?'

'I'll show you,' said Rebecca. 'I need to go myself.'

Jill stood up, swayed slightly, said, 'See you in a bit', to Harry and went off with Rebecca, who turned to her and began to talk as soon as they were away from the table.

'So you're a pal of Leo Shapiro's, then,' said Norris.

'I've known him quite a while,' admitted Harry.

'He's a lucky bastard,' said Fieldhouse. 'I mean he's the luckiest bastard I know. Here's us out here 'cause of what the Old Bill's got written up against our names, and there's him sitting pretty in the middle of fucking London town. Can do what he likes and nobody takes the blindest bit of notice.'

'That's not luck,' said Norris. 'That's being clever.'

'So he's a clever bastard. That still makes him the luckiest clever bastard I know.'

Harry had to agree with both views of Shapiro, who had certainly been lucky but, then again, had always been careful. The authorities were always more likely to live and let live with

46

the Shapiros of this world, who knew what the limit was and stayed within it, than with the kind of reckless hot-head that Fieldhouse seemed to be, always liable to end up killing somebody.

'He's also a good friend of ours,' said Norris. 'Let's not forget that, shall we?' It wasn't so much a testimonial as a warning.

Fieldhouse seemed to get the message and said nothing, concentrating on refilling his glass. Harry was glad Jill had been out of the way while the character of their benefactor had taken such a mauling. He silently vowed that next time they'd travel with Cooks or Thompsons, somebody with offices in the high street who wouldn't land them in the company of villains.

'He's all right is Leo,' said Norris.

''Course he is,' said Mullins.

'I'm not saying he isn't,' said Fieldhouse sullenly. 'Just that he's lucky.'

'Nothing wrong with that. They're the people you want to know, the ones that always turn out lucky.'

'He's got a funny wife, though,' said Sam. 'I mean you can hardly get her to touch a drink and then it's just the one sherry.'

The waiter returned to remove their plates. Mullins took his sleeve and said something quietly to him, at which the boy smiled and said, '*Si.*'

'And what time will you finish?'

He made a gesture of helplessness and indicated the crowded tables around them. 'Could be one, two . . . any time.'

The two women returned. Rebecca had pulled her hair back into a pony-tail. Jill gave Harry a smile and sat down deliberately with the air of one who knew she'd had too much to drink and wasn't going to let it show.

Norris made an announcement. 'Now tomorrow night, everybody comes to my place, right? We'll have a party.'

'I thought all this was one long party,' said Rebecca.

'Yes well, tomorrow it's at my place. That all right for you, Harry? You two'll be there, won't you?'

'Yes, I suppose . . . ' said Harry, and looked to Jill.

'Thank you,' she said meekly.

'Terrific. We'll get some food. It'll make a change from this dump.'

'You mean I'll get some food,' said Rebecca.

'That's what I meant, yes, my darling. You get us some food. Now is anybody ready for another bottle? I know that piss-artist there will be.'

'I am,' said Fieldhouse.

'That's it, yes, piss-artist,' agreed Sam.

Fieldhouse gripped her wrist. 'Just watch it, eh?'

She gave a squeal of pain. 'You're hurting!'

'Then just be careful of that mouth of yours,' he said, letting go.

'She's saying you're a piss-artist. What's wrong with that?' said Norris.

'Nothing. I just don't want her saying it, that's all.'

'I'd quite like a coffee if there's one going,' said Jill.

'Sure,' said Harry, welcoming the opportunity to move from the table and stretch his legs. 'Anybody else?'

Rebecca said she'd also like one, and Harry went to the bar and ordered three coffees, one for himself. When he returned, Rebecca was instructing Jill on places she should visit – Mijas, Cordoba, Granada. Sam was sulking and Fieldhouse and Mullins were talking about the price of an Audi sports coupé they both fancied.

'You'll come tomorrow, then, Harry?' said Norris.

'Come to . . . ?'

'To my place. Tomorrow night.'

'Oh, yes. Sure.'

'Alan, you'll be all right?'

Mullins said he was.

'Gerald?'

'Course.'

Sam he didn't bother to ask. Either Fieldhouse spoke for both or Norris couldn't give a damn whether she turned up or not.

'Tell you what, Harry, the best thing will be if one of us comes and collects you. It'll be easier than giving directions.'

Harry agreed. Why not? If they were going anyway, which they seemed committed to doing, it could hardly matter how they got there. Around them the tables were beginning to clear.

'Can we go?' Jill asked quietly. 'I'm tired.'

'You go, my love,' said Norris, overhearing. 'Don't worry about this lot. They'll be here till the place closes.'

'It's a tradition,' said Rebecca sardonically. 'About the only one we've got.'

'And then Alan's got to wait for Luigi to finish, haven't you, Alan?'

Mullins gave a shy smile. 'Somebody has to see he gets home in one piece.'

'Well, we'll see you then,' said Harry, helping Jill to her feet. 'And thanks for the help earlier.' He was assured it had been a pleasure, which was no doubt true. 'Now what about the bill . . . ?' he began, but was silenced by an imperious Norris, who said he wasn't to worry about the bill – that was all taken care of. Rebecca nodded in agreement, so he said thanks and left it at that. They departed to a chorus of good-nights and instructions to sleep well. It was a small surprise to move away from the table and the music and realise they'd been outdoors all the time. The sky above was now black save for a three-quarter moon that yielded a little light for their journey home.

They walked slowly, their arms around one another.

'I quite like her really,' said Jill, sounding drowsy.

'Who?'

'Rebecca. Oh, not Sam. God, she's a tart. But Rebecca, she's . . . well, she's not taken in. She knows what they're all like and isn't fooled by any of them.'

'No,' agreed Harry, relieved to find Jill approving of the other woman without knowing why it should have mattered.

'She was talking to me. When we went to the loo. Apparently they're all scared to death about this Tommy Smith business.'

Harry had to think back. 'This mate of theirs who's disappeared?'

'Yes. They don't really believe he's just gone off somewhere without telling them. That was just . . . just . . . '

'For our benefit.'

'Yes. They really think he's been killed.'

He didn't know which was the more surprising, what he was hearing or the fact he was hearing it from Jill, who suddenly seemed to be taking such fearful revelations in her stride. At which point she stumbled and was only saved by his arm around her.

'Oops, sorry,' she said. 'I'm pissed.'

'It's dark.'

'It might be dark. I'm still pissed.'

They arrived at their gate. Harry unlocked it and then locked it again behind them.

'They think he might have got involved with some local drug-trafficking and that's what's got him killed.'

'This is Tommy Smith . . . ?'

'Yes. Either that or the English police have abducted him.'

'I didn't know they went in for that kind of game,' said Harry, taken aback. He knew some of the behind-the-scenes games the English police occasionally played but none that included kidnapping from foreign territories.

'It's what Rebecca says. But Norris thinks he's probably been killed.' They arrived in the bedroom. Jill unceremoniously pulled off her clothes and collapsed on to the bed. 'God, I am pissed. I'm sorry, Harry.'

'Don't be,' he said, amused.

'Have I said anything awful?'

'No. You've been wonderful. As always.'

'I don't feel it.' She kicked off the duvet, leaving a single sheet. 'I feel hot.'

'It is hot. I'll open some windows.'

'They're wondering who'll be next. That's what they're so scared about. Who might be the next to be killed after Tommy Smith.'

And she fell asleep.

5.

Harry's first move the following morning, while Jill was still sleeping, was to sneak another look at the photograph of the five men boozing together at the Café Ricco. Shapiro he could have identified from the age of sixteen; three more were now known to him from last night; therefore the fifth must be the missing Tommy Smith. From what could be seen of him from behind his raised glass, he looked a biggish man running to fat, with a podgy face, light-coloured hair and small moustache.

The second thing he did was to take another nerve-tingling plunge into the pool and swim off his faint headache, the legacy of last night's drinking.

He'd fixed himself coffee and toast by the time Jill emerged, looking drawn and fragile.

'Morning,' he said cheerily.

'Good morning.'

'All right?'

'No, I'm not. Why did I drink so much?'

'Because you're on holiday,' he said, seeking to make a joke of it.

But she wasn't amused. 'It was because I didn't know what else to do. In that company I didn't know what else to do. Because I was right, wasn't I? When I said they'd all turn out to be criminals, I was right.'

'Have a coffee. Don't worry about it.'

'How can I not worry about it?'

'All right, worry if it makes you happy. But have a coffee anyway.'

'Harry, it's not funny.'

'No. Sorry.' He tried to keep a straight face but it slipped into a grin, which infected Jill till she, too, couldn't prevent a smile. 'Come here,' he said, and they embraced.

'Promise me one thing, though, Harry.'

'Anything.'

'We aren't going to have to spend the whole holiday with them, are we?'

'Of course we're not.'

'I couldn't stand that.'

'You won't have to. Now, how're you feeling?'

'Terrible.'

No need yet to remind her of their promise to attend Norris's party that evening. Let her revive first and then choose the right moment. 'Have a swim,' he suggested. 'It'll do you good.' But she winced at the thought, so he left her alone, content to sit and soak up the sun while she returned into the villa. He heard the sound of a bath being run.

By midday she was feeling brighter, and they went and established themselves on the beach. Harry bought some cokes and a hamburger to supplement his meagre breakfast.

'Do you mind if I don't look at you while you're eating that?' she said, turning away.

'Don't mind at all.'

'You must have a stomach made of iron.'

Along the beach the sand-sculptor had arrived and was engaged in a vigorous series of press-ups before embarking on his day's work. There was a smell of cooking from the ramshackle bar-restaurant and a constant drone of distant traffic from the coastal road that divided the strip of beach from the hill-side villa developments.

'Do I remember,' said Jill slowly and still gazing away from him out to sea, 'that we're supposed to be going out with them again tonight?'

'Not exactly . . . '

'Thank God for that.'

'But we did say we'd go round to Norris's. He's giving some sort of party.'

'I knew there was something,' she said quietly.

'We can leave as soon as you like,' said Harry, finishing his hamburger. 'Don't have to go at all if you don't want to.

52

Though, to be honest, I thought you were quite enjoying yourself last night.' He wondered what to do with the paper serviette that had come with the hamburger and stuffed it into the pocket of his shorts. 'By the way, I've finished eating. I mean in case you want to look round.'

She didn't move but asked, 'And wasn't there something about one of them being killed?'

'Not killed exactly,' he said, lowering his voice lest they should be overheard. 'There's a friend of theirs been missing for a few weeks, that's all.'

But she wasn't so easily reassured and turned to face him. 'Tommy Smith.'

'Yes.'

'I remember now. Rebecca was telling me. They think he's been killed. I probably didn't tell you. She says Norris is practically certain he's been killed and is scared to death it might be somebody out to get all of them.'

'You did tell me.'

'Did I?'

'Yes.'

'Oh well, then perhaps you'll understand why I'm not so desperate to spend all our holiday with these people.'

'I've told you. We don't have to. Do you want some oil on your back?'

'I suppose I'd better.'

He started to apply it; then she said something he couldn't hear since she was speaking into her towel.

'What?'

'I said what crimes did they commit in England, do you know?'

'No idea.'

'So it could have been anything. Could have been mugging old ladies.'

'I doubt it.' The mugging of banks or warehouses, yes, but not senior citizens. Though whether Jill would regard this as more or less culpable he didn't know and so didn't suggest it. 'Do you fancy a walk?' he asked.

'Not really,' she said, yawning. 'But you go if you like. Don't let me stop you.'

Porto Banus was a prestigious seafront development a mile or so along the beach. Harry, growing impatient after another half-hour of idleness, took Jill at her word and strolled off alone to investigate it.

No old fishing-village this but a modern complex of white apartments huddled around an extensive marina chock-a-block with yachts and motor-launches of all shapes and sizes but mostly in the large to enormous category. Some, indeed, were more like small ocean-going liners, with multiple decks hung with lifeboats and topped by elaborate radar-dishes. Harry joined the tourists wandering the jetties and gaping at the display of assembled floating palaces.

He stopped before one of the largest, whose deck led to glass doors through which could be glimpsed a state-room in which twelve people might have comfortably sat down to dinner. A young Arabian-looking man descended from an upper deck and came down a small gangplank to the quayside. He was casually dressed and wore mirror sunglasses. Affecting not to notice the display of interest among the by-standers, he climbed into a yellow Rolls-Royce Corniche that was parked there and drove away.

Harry remembered what Jill had said – that the missing Tommy Smith might have been involved in drug-trafficking. Certainly it wasn't far from here across the Med to Morocco, and no Customs power on earth could keep an effective check on such an armada.

'Thinking of buying one, then?' said a voice behind him.

It was Rebecca. He knew immediately, even before he turned and saw her, and he knew, too, something else: that here was a woman he fancied and fancied strongly, the first time this had happened since he'd met Jill and they'd thrown in their lot with one another.

'No,' he smiled. 'Just looking.'

'So am I. Only it's the owners I'm looking for. Well, just one would do. So long as he was single and hetero and didn't expect me to climb the yard-arm and all that crap.'

Harry laughed, though she didn't seem to be joking. Perhaps she really did parade here daily looking for a millionaire pickup. She was wearing tight Bermuda shorts and a cream tee-shirt that this time had nothing written across it to distract from her figure.

'I don't know what a yard-arm is,' admitted Harry.

'I do but I'm not going to tell you. Where's Jill?'

'On the beach. Still recovering from last night.'

'Ah well, it's a hard life if you're not used to it,' she said and took his arm. 'So I've got you to myself, have I?'

Harry made no reply beyond a small laugh, and they began to stroll together past the open fronts of the restaurants and bars and boutiques that faced the marina.

'This is the posiest place on earth,' said Rebecca, 'and one of the most expensive. Anything you want to buy here you let me know and I'll show you where you can get it for half the price.'

'How about a drink?' he said. 'And something to eat?'

'OK,' she agreed and, true to her promise, directed him away from the ritzy estabishments lining the marina, where crystal glass shone on white damask and the prices were figures casually plucked out of the air, to a smallish bar round the back that was cheaper and cosier. It pleased and flattered him when they entered to a small stir among the nautical-looking males draped along the bar as they spotted Rebecca. This is dangerous, he thought. I shouldn't be alone with this woman. Even more dangerous was that he wasn't alarmed at all but was excited, grateful now that Jill had been too lazy to accompany him but had stayed where she was on her towel.

'I don't want to eat,' said Rebecca, 'but don't let that put you off.'

So he ordered a sandwich for himself and beer for both of them.

'Aren't you working?' he asked.

She shook her head. 'Days off. And anyway I'm sick to death of the bloody job. It's time I had a change. Time

I changed a lot of things.'

'And where's Norris?' he asked, hoping it would be some-where far away.

'Norris?' It was as though she needed a moment to remember who he was. 'Oh, out and about. Keeping fit. Seeing his lawyer. Doing his laundry. I'm not all that interested.'

'Oh,' said Harry, not sure what sort of response this called for.

She laughed. 'Don't worry. *I'm* not going to kill him. Just that I've been seeing him for a while and . . . well, you get bored with people, don't you?'

'Sometimes,' he said guardedly.

'Well, I do. I'd have been bored last night if you hadn't been there.'

There was a pause. Harry allowed his gaze to wander round the bar till he found a safer topic for conversation. 'I suppose what Norris said last night, that's all true, is it? I mean about him and the other two – they really are out here on the run?'

'Oh sure,' she said without hesitation. 'They've been out here about eighteen months. They worked together on a big jewel robbery in Bond Street. London's Bond Street.'

'Yes,' he said. 'I know it.'

'They got away with about half-a-million quid's worth of diamonds.'

'And then what happened?'

'Well, Norris doesn't know for sure. Perhaps Fieldhouse got pissed and talked too much. Though, of course, he says he didn't. But something went wrong somewhere. Norris got word from a contact of his in Scotland Yard that they'd been rumbled and were going to be picked up. So, rather than wait and see, they all took the first boat to Calais, then hired a car and didn't stop driving till they got down here.'

Harry thought about it. 'If they took half-a-million quid's worth of jewellery . . . '

'Yes?'

'Well, they'd have to fence that, so they'd end up with perhaps half its value.'

'Something like that.'

'And is that what they're living on, the three of them?'

The sum didn't add up. If the style of Shapiro's villa was any guide to the standard of living being enjoyed by the rest, then the income from a few trays of Bond Street gems should be about exhausted by now, with only coppers left for binges like last night's.

But Rebecca explained. 'Oh, not just that, no. Norris has a lot more tucked away from earlier jobs. He has this trust fund on the Channel Islands under some name or other, and God knows what else he has besides.'

'That's all come from other jobs?'

'Oh yes. That jeweller wasn't his first not by a long chalk.'

'He's told you all about them, has he?' said Harry, curious about the relationship between these two as well as a touch concerned at the way Rebecca seemed happy to spell out her lover's criminal c.v. to a relative stranger like himself. It struck him that Norris wouldn't be too pleased if he knew of the way she airily broadcast his exploits.

'He never stops telling me,' she said. 'The first time I thought it was fantastic. Well, that's what turned me on. It's why I slept with him. The second time it was still interesting. That's why I slept with him again. Now it's boring. So perhaps it's time I started sleeping with somebody else. What do you think?'

And she forced him to look into those hazel eyes of hers and put one hand on his where it lay on the table. There was an invitation there that couldn't be ignored, though whether she was teasing or serious . . . well, it didn't bear thinking about. He removed his hand on the pretext of having to pick up his glass.

'What about the other two, Fieldhouse and Mullins?'

'I haven't slept with them, no. I wouldn't touch that pig Fieldhouse with a barge-pole and I don't think I've got the right sort of equipment to interest Alan.'

Harry smiled and said patiently, 'I meant how're they fixed financially?'

'Oh, that's what you meant.'

57

'That's what I meant.'

'Well, I'm not sure. But I wouldn't think either of them is rolling in it. Certainly nothing like Norris is. See, they'd only worked on a couple of jobs with him, and anyway he was in charge and took the lion's share.'

'But they'd done other jobs before, had they?'

'So I gather. I don't know what, though. Norris only talks about himself. He's got this pile of press-cuttings in the bedroom. Articles about the different jobs he's done.'

'He's got them with him over here?'

'Yes. Remind me and I'll show you them tonight.'

Harry gave a little laugh. 'I'm not sure Norris would be too keen on you doing that.'

She looked him in the eye. 'I hoped one thing I'd made clear was that I'm not very interested in what Norris wants. I'm not very interested in Norris any more.'

'Well . . . yes.'

'So I'll see you in the bedroom, then.'

'It's a date,' he said solemnly, wondering which of them was joking. If either. Of course, it was still possible Jill would put her foot down and they wouldn't be going at all. Even if they did, the opportunity to be alone with Rebecca was unlikely to arise. Unfortunately.

'So what about Tommy Smith? Where does he fit into all this?'

'Oh, he didn't work with Norris. At least I don't think so. He was wanted for some big fraud or other, I don't know the details. Only he'd known Norris in the past and so when Norris arrived over here he helped him with buying a property, things like that.'

'And then he went missing.'

'Yes. Did Jill tell you they're afraid somebody might have knocked him off?'

'Yes.'

'There were rumours about him being involved in some kind of local drug-dealing. I once asked Norris about it and he told me to mind my own business, which probably means they were true. And he certainly used drugs himself, as well as the booze.' She paused, then added reflectively, 'It's par for the course with a lot that come to live over here. I mean even your honest citizens. There's nothing to do but get high on one thing or another. And Tommy wasn't even your honest citizen to start with.'

'So what do you think has happened to him?'

She shrugged. 'Don't know. I don't think anybody misses him much, except for maybe Norris. What they're really worried about is that if the police here get interested then it might stir things up for everybody else.'

'You mean get them thrown out . . . ? Deported . . . ?'

'Yes. Undesirable aliens and all that.'

Harry asked if she wanted another drink, and she said no. Since he didn't either, they left the bar and sauntered back past the lines of boats. At the end of the quayside was a stone seat, where Rebecca sat down. 'There's room for you,' she said, seeing he hadn't moved to join her.

He hesitated, glancing at his watch. 'Yes, I was just wondering . . . ' he muttered. Most of the afternoon had already gone. Then he thought what the hell, Jill could look after herself. Rebecca looked more luscious than ever, settling herself like a cat in the sun before him. He sat down beside her, trying to keep a decent gap between them on the narrow bench.

'Isn't there supposed to be a new extradition treaty between Britain and Spain?' he asked. 'I thought I read about it somewhere.'

'There's one on the cards,' she said, her eyes closed. 'It's been on the cards ever since they joined the Common Market but it hasn't been passed by the Spanish parliament yet.'

'And so what happens when it is passed?'

'Well, nobody knows for sure. I mean it'll certainly stop anybody else on the run coming over here but what it'll do to those already here is anybody's guess.'

'So they're worrying about that, too, are they?'

'Well, Norris claims there shouldn't be any problem because apparently the Spanish constitution states that laws can't be

59

applied retrospectively.' When Harry didn't immediately respond, she opened one eye and said, 'That means what they've done already doesn't count.'

'I know what it means. So Norris and the gang would be all right because they were here before the new law was passed.'

'That's what he's hoping.'

'And what if he's wrong?'

'If he's wrong . . . well, I suppose he'll try and take off for somewhere else. Costa Rica, North Africa . . . somewhere where the natives are friendlier. Though whether the other two could afford to do the same . . . ' She sounded doubtful.

'Their funds wouldn't run to it?'

She nodded. 'I suspect – just suspect, mind you – that they don't have an awful lot of pesetas left.'

'Can't they work over here?'

'You mean legitimate, regular employment, that sort of work?'

'Yes.'

'No way. That'd get 'em deported even quicker than if they started thieving again.'

If this were paradise, as Fieldhouse had claimed, then it was beginning to sound dangerously insecure. Both he and Mullins were condemned to enforced idleness while the last of their money seeped away. And even Norris, with his Channel Islands trust funds behind him, had the worry of what might happen when the British–Spanish extradition treaty was finally ratified, to say nothing of what might have already happened to his friend Tommy Smith. Though perhaps even a flawed paradise was preferable to ten years in the nick.

The Arab in the yellow Corniche had returned and went up the gangplank of his sumptuous yacht, where he was greeted affectionately by two girls in bikinis. He accepted their welcome as his due, then proceeded through the glass doors into the state-room, leaving them to follow.

'And so you're looking for your millionaire to take you away from all this?' said Harry lightly.

'Yes.' She spoke seriously. 'He wouldn't have to take me

away, though. Just let me give up this crappy job I've got.'

'Well, best of luck.'

'Thanks.'

He looked again at his watch, then climbed reluctantly to his feet. 'I'd better be getting back. See you tonight.'

She looked up at him, shading her eyes against the sun. 'Did you notice me watching you last night? When we were at the café?'

'Now and again,' he admitted.

'I was looking at you and your lady. You make an odd couple, you know that?'

He found her observation disconcerting in its accuracy. They were an odd couple, of course – Jill, born in the Home Counties and educated at Lady Margaret College, Oxford, while he'd come from Mile End and learned most of what he knew in Wormwood Scrubs. But he didn't enjoy being reminded of it by Rebecca of all people.

He shrugged. 'Most couples are odd, aren't they?'

'No. Most are understandable. You and her aren't.'

He felt compelled to retaliate. 'And where does that leave you and Norris? I'd have thought you made an unlikely twosome if anybody did.'

She gave a wry smile. 'Touché. Only, like I said, forget about Norris. He doesn't figure in future plans.'

'Poor Norris.'

'I shouldn't think he'll be heart-broken.'

'I would be.'

He'd intended only a mild compliment. Now, hearing himself say it, it sounded more like a declaration.

Rebecca smiled. 'Would you, now?'

'Anyway,' he said, 'see you tonight.'

'*Ciao*,' she called after him as he went away.

It promised to be an interesting, not to say fraught, evening. The more he discovered about the small ex-pat community, the more they sounded less like a privileged élite and more like a ghetto under siege. While the more he discovered about himself, the more he was amazed to find his feeling for Jill under siege.

61

He marched back along the beach. Come on, he told himself, Rebecca might be attractive, sexy, inviting even, but he was committed to Jill. They lived together. They would continue to do so after this holiday was over and forgotten. Rebecca was committed to finding herself a millionaire who'd stake her to the good life. She probably flirted with everybody in the way that she had flirted with him that afternoon.

What he should do was tell Jill they weren't going to Norris's party and suggest they have a romantic evening alone instead. That was what he should do, but he knew already that he wouldn't.

6.

Norris's villa was two and a half miles from Shapiro's as the crow flew. Somewhat further on a road that wound this way and that as it rose into the hills. As promised, transport was provided for Jill and Harry in the shape of Alan Mullins driving a grey Citroën.

'So how's the old holiday going, then?' asked Mullins once they were under way.

'Fine, yes. Great,' said Harry.

Jill, sitting beside him in the back seat, lit a cigarette and stared out at the increasingly desolate landscape. They had left behind them the cheek-by-jowl development of the coastal strip; what buildings there were up here were dotted randomly about the hill-sides, one or two half-finished and abandoned-looking.

'Here we are,' announced Mullins. 'That's Norris's pad over there.'

They looked and saw a huddled compound. Pink masonry could be glimpsed through the trees.

'How long has he lived there?' asked Jill.

'Oh, must be three or four years now. Perhaps longer.'

There were other cars already parked. The boundaries of the garden were marked by the standard iron fence, for good measure topped by strands of barbed wire. Entering it, they saw that the building was indeed pink and the garden extensive, boasting a swimming-pool with a fountain at each corner. Norris came to meet them and shook hands.

'Good to see you again, Harry. And you, darling.'

The interior was not unlike the one they had just left: marbled floors and cream-coloured walls, with the same rather sparse, lightweight furniture. As if both Norris and Leo Shapiro had bought job-lots from the same warehouse. A dozen people were already present, standing around with drinks in their

63

hands. Gerald Fieldhouse and Samantha were sitting together on a sofa. Seeing Harry, Fieldhouse raised a hand in salute, and Samantha gave a tired smile.

Norris ushered them through to the kitchen where bottles and glasses were ranged. 'Now help yourselves, won't you? And don't be frightened of it. There's plenty more where that came from.' He set the example by pouring a generous measure of vodka into his own glass.

'I'll just have a Perrier water,' said Jill firmly.

'Suit yourself, darling. By the way, I see you're a fast learner.'

'Pardon?'

'Haven't brought your handbag with you tonight, have you? Getting to know the ways of this effing country.' He laughed to show he was joking. 'No, don't you worry. You'll be all right tonight. Everybody leaves their guns at the door when they come in here.' Another laugh, in which Jill hesitantly shared. 'Right, I think we want some music. Get everybody wakened up. 'Scuse me while I go and stick a tape on.' And he left them to their own devices.

The music, when it came, was from Manitas de Plata but did little to lighten the subdued atmosphere. Everybody seemed on their best behaviour, not sure why they had been summoned. Norris was an energetic, even bullying host, wandering among them with his vodka bottle and urging them to drink more.

Rebecca was outside in the garden, talking in Spanish to a silvery-haired man who had a young girl on his arm who might have been his daughter or his mistress. She glanced round as Harry and Jill approached, giving them a smile which took in both and a rather off-hand 'Hi' before resuming her conversation. Harry felt faintly slighted though couldn't have said what more he'd expected. He caught a whiff of her perfume as they passed.

Later they were collared by Norris and taken to meet some people standing together in the lounge. 'This is Harry and Jill, friends of mine from London,' he said belligerently as if challenging anyone to deny it. 'This is Helga and Heinz. And

Mats and Kerstin. Now everybody has a drink, haven't they? And don't forget to eat. There's a great load of nosh we have to get through.'

Helga and Heinz were an elderly couple from Munich who had retired from there to become near-neighbours of Norris. 'Just there, over the hill,' they said, indicating the general direction of their villa.

Mats and Kerstin were Swedish hairdressers with a shop in Marbella.

'This sun is doing terrible things to my hair,' said Jill, raising a hand to it. 'I must come and see you.'

'Any time,' said Mats politely. 'It would be a pleasure.'

'I'm starving,' said Harry, noticing Rebecca had come in from outside and was at the dining-table. 'Can I get anything for anybody else?'

Jill said she wouldn't mind a small plateful, and so he moved away from the group to the dining-table where there was a spread of cold meats and salads. It brought him close to Rebecca, whose smile this time had a more personal, intimate edge to it.

'And how're you?' she said.

'Fine. You look terrific.'

She was wearing white jeans and a crimson halter top. Also make-up and jewellery, which made her look older, more self-aware than the child of sea and sand she'd previously seemed to be.

'Thank you,' she said.

'Great food, too.'

She laughed. 'I can't take the credit for that. There's a place along the coast that delivers. I just placed the order and they did the rest.' Then, seeing he had a plate in each hand: 'Here, let me help you.' And she piled on the food, every inch the eager hostess to Norris's jovial host.

'Thanks,' he said, when the plates were full and he'd no longer the excuse for lingering. 'I'll see you later.'

'You certainly will,' she said, looking him in the eye.

He returned to Jill, who was talking to the German couple.

Heinz, it appeared, had been a lawyer before his retirement, and now his conversation with Jill had reached the same topic as had Harry's with Rebecca that afternoon – the question of extradition and how the new bill going through the Spanish parliament might change things.

'It will not be retrospective,' Harry caught him saying as he handed Jill her food. 'But, of course, everything depends on how that is interpreted by the courts.'

'How do you mean?' asked Jill.

'Well, let us say that someone has committed a crime in England and has then come over here to escape from its consequences. Like our good friend Norris for example.' Indicating the burly figure.

'Yes.'

'And let's say the British authorities have issued a warrant for his arrest; but because there was no extradition treaty until now, that has been the end of it. And still nothing will happen after this new law is passed. Because it will not apply to the old warrant, and so the fugitive is safe.'

'Absolutely.'

'But – and this is the question – what will happen if the British authorities issue a new warrant? Will that be regarded as retrospective by the Spanish courts? Or will they accept it as new and therefore act on it?'

'Oh, I see,' said Jill. 'And what do you think?'

'I have no idea. Like I say, only the courts can decide.'

Norris arrived with a bottle of red wine in one hand and a bottle of white in the other. 'Come on, you can drink and talk at the same time,' he said, refilling Heinz's glass.

'We were talking about the courts' attitude towards extradition,' said Heinz, chuckling.

'Don't talk to me about sodding courts,' said Norris. 'They've never done me any favours, not the English ones anyway.'

'Perhaps the Spanish ones will be more sympathetic,' said Heinz.

'I wouldn't put money on it,' said Norris, coming to Jill's glass.

'Now, darling, what are you, red or white?'

'Neither. It's Perrier water.'

'Fair enough. No, the thing about you lawyers, Heinz my old son, is that you think all this court-room stuff is dead interesting as well as being highly rewarding. Which maybe it is to you. But to the man in the dock it's not quite such a big joke, you know what I mean?'

'I never joke,' objected Heinz. 'Every case I ever fought was life or death to me.'

'I'm sure it was. 'Cept if you cocked it up it wasn't you that got sent down, was it? Now don't get me going about lawyers, Heinz, because you know I hate 'em. Present company excepted.'

'We're not all that bad, surely,' said Heinz, amused.

'You're a pack of sodding vultures,' said Norris. 'Now enjoy yourself. I don't want anybody going home sober, all right?' And he moved away towards Fieldhouse and Sam, who were still on the sofa.

Obviously he didn't mind his fate being the general topic of conversation among his guests, thought Harry. No doubt he enjoyed the lime-light, the feeling of being a celebrity out here among the holiday-makers and retired lawyers.

Heinz still hadn't finished worrying away at the legal niceties. 'Let's suppose the British authorities are even cleverer,' he went on. 'So that when they issue a new warrant they make it a little different from the original one. Alter the charge. Even reduce it to a more minor one – knowing that they can return to the original charge once they have the accused back in England.'

Jill seemed as fascinated by the topic as he was. 'You mean if they did that, then the Spanish courts would be more likely to accept it?'

'Well, no-one knows till there's been a test case. But it would be more difficult to defend.'

She thought of a further complication.

'Anyone coming to Spain after the new law is passed will certainly be liable to extradition, won't they?'

'Oh yes. It's only with those already in residence here that the problems arise.'

'So what if somebody already resident – like Norris – left Spain and then returned to it? Suppose they crossed the border to Portugal or Gibraltar for a holiday? Or even for a day's shopping. Would that make them liable to extradition on the grounds that their residency hadn't been continuous?'

'You should have been a lawyer,' said Heinz, smiling. 'Yes, it might well. That is, of course, if it could be proved that they actually had crossed the border and then returned.'

'Or even, say, gone for a sail and ended up outside Spanish territorial waters?'

Heinz pondered that one. 'Interesting,' he said. 'It would be harder to prove but . . . well, it would make an intriguing case.'

'So if you picked the wrong day to go sailing,' said Jill, 'you might find yourself in a gale-force wind and, before you knew where you were, you'd have been blown back into an English jail!'

Heinz laughed. 'Yes. Blown by the wind into an English jail. Oh yes, I like that!'

He was probably right, thought Harry. Jill would have made a good lawyer. She was always telling him she wasn't patient enough for teaching and certainly enjoyed the kind of abstract argument with all its ifs and buts that she and Heinz were now pursuing. He wondered, too, how far it was this intelligence of hers, and the bits of paper she had to prove it, that helped bind him to her, making him feel the inferior partner, the one who should be grateful.

Around them the party began to liven up. Harry went to the kitchen to replenish his glass and walked in on a row between Fieldhouse and Samantha, who had finally moved from their sofa.

'You stupid bitch . . . ' Fieldhouse was saying, then stopped when he saw Harry. 'All right then, Harry boy?'

'Yes.'

'You wouldn't believe this. I'm just telling her' – meaning Samantha who was helping herself to a tumblerful of *vino* –

'that we're planning on a carding session for later and so she can take herself off home. And what does she do but start throwing a fucking tantrum.'

'Piss off,' muttered Samantha.

He grabbed a handful of her hair. 'You what? What was that again?'

She kicked out and caught him on the shins. 'Bitch,' he said, and pushed her hard so that, caught off balance, she was thrown across the kitchen, hitting a cupboard with a jarring thud. She gave a cry of pain, then looked round in search of a weapon. 'Just watch who you're fucking kicking,' said Fieldhouse. She grabbed her glass of wine and threw it. It struck Fieldhouse on the shoulder and fell to the floor without breaking but splattered him and a fair area of the kitchen with its contents. Then she turned and ran from the room before he could counter-attack.

Fieldhouse produced a string of muttered obscenities and tried to dash away the wine that was staining his shirt. 'What the hell can you do with 'em?' he asked Harry in despair. 'Fucking maniacs.'

Rebecca appeared in the doorway.

'Just what are you playing at?' she demanded, and then saw the mess. 'Oh Christ, Gerald.'

'I didn't do nothing,' he protested. 'It's that stupid bitch. She's wrong in her head.'

'I don't know why you can't just kill one another and get it over with,' said Rebecca. She threw him a cloth. 'Wipe up that mess, will you? Norris is in a foul enough mood as it is.'

'Why?' asked Harry.

'Oh, God knows. Except that he's been gargling with vodka since about five o'clock, which is always guaranteed to turn him even more unpleasant than he normally is. Anyway, didn't we have a date?' She took his hand. 'Come on.'

She pulled him from the kitchen, leaving Fieldhouse with the cloth. The lounge had become crowded with people who had wandered in from the garden, which was now in darkness save for the underwater lights of the swimming-pool.

'I'm just borrowing him a minute,' Rebecca called as they passed Jill.

'Be my guest,' she said.

They went into one of the bedrooms. Rebecca closed the door firmly, then turned to face him.

'There,' she said. 'Easy, wasn't it?'

'Easy getting in,' he admitted. 'I'm not so sure how we get out.'

'Oh, you want to get out?' she said, and stood aside as though to let him pass.

'No,' he said and shook his head. 'Oh no.'

There was a tantalising moment, then he stepped towards her, took her in his arms and kissed her. Her response was immediate and eager, then she pulled away.

'Mustn't forget what we're here for,' she said quietly.

'I thought this was it,' he protested.

But she stepped back, allowing her fingertips to trail the palms of his hands as they parted, then moved to the other side of the bed where she stooped and opened a bedside cabinet.

'Here we are,' she said, and pulled out what looked like a photograph-album. 'Norris's press-cuttings.'

'Oh,' said Harry. 'Of course.'

'Well, come on, Harry,' she said. 'I mean there are about three million people on the other side of that door. Who all might come walking in at any minute. And you did say you'd like to see Norris's collection.'

'I suppose I did. Though right now it doesn't seem all that exciting.'

'There's a time and place for everything,' she said. 'And, quite honestly, I don't think this is it.'

Harry gave a grunt of reluctant agreement. 'But what if Norris comes in and finds me looking at this?' he said, picking up the album. 'I can't see him being too happy about that.'

She shook her head. 'He wouldn't care.'

'No?'

'No. He'd probably insist on talking you through them. He likes showing them to people. I've seen him.'

70

'Strange man.'

'Oh, he's that all right.'

He opened the album, which was intended for photographs but which was full of newspaper cuttings, one to each page. At the top of the page was printed the date and the name of the newspaper from which it had been taken.

A quick flick through gave Harry an impression of bold headlines with words such as 'ROBBERY' and 'THIEVES' strongly featured. Most were from the Sunday press or the tabloids, though the occasional small column was headed DAILY TELEGRAPH or TIMES.

'He reckons to have more at home in England,' said Rebecca, 'but that's the only one he has over here with him.' As he had sat on the bed to study the album she had come to stand next to him, her thigh provocatively close. 'Have a proper read through them if you like. Don't mind me.'

'You've got to be joking.'

'Would you like me to leave the room?'

'No. Just don't stand quite so close.'

She laughed. 'Am I stopping you concentrating?'

'You're stopping me breathing.'

She went and sat before the dressing-table. Harry turned the album over so that he was again looking at the front and began a more leisurely survey of its contents. The first pages of articles all featured a bank robbery in Chelmsford. 'DAYLIGHT BANK HOLD-UP' (DAILY EXPRESS). 'MASKED BANK RAID' (THE SUN). They told how four men, two armed with shotguns, had raided a high-street branch of Barclays Bank. Estimates of their haul varied from eighty thousand to a hundred and thirty thousand pounds, but all the accounts told of the threats made to customers and staff, who had been forced to lie on the floor. A woman customer had had to gag her small child, who had started yelling and couldn't be silenced.

Other articles told of a series of raids on sub-post offices, seven or eight of them at locations scattered across the south-east of England. 'POSTAL RAIDERS STRIKE AGAIN' (THE STAR). Each time the *modus operandi* had been the same: a late-night break-in by two men and the terrorising of the occupiers of the shop premises, who'd been made to hand over the keys before being tied up and gagged. 'NIGHT OF TERROR FOR POSTMASTER AND WIFE' (NEWS OF THE WORLD). In one case the shopkeeper had resisted and been beaten up; another had suffered a heart attack and been resuscitated by policemen called to the scene.

'Enjoying it?' asked Rebecca.

'Not a lot. Seems like he was a real nutter once upon a time, was our friend Norris.'

'He still is. People don't change, do they? And Norris is still one-hundred-per-cent certifiable when he feels like it.'

A final batch of articles told about the raid on the Bond Street jeweller that Rebecca had already mentioned. 'GEMS HAUL FOR SHOTGUN RAIDERS' (MAIL ON SUNDAY). A blue Ford Transit van had been driven up on to the pavement so that it blocked the entrance to the up-market Bond Street shop. Three men had then rushed in, all masked and one armed with a shotgun with which he threatened to 'blow out the brains of anybody that moved' (THE SUN). He had held at bay the two members of staff and the one customer present while his two colleagues swept trays of rings, bracelets and necklaces into the plastic bin-liners they were carrying. The whole operation had taken no more than fifteen or twenty seconds before the three men were out again and making their getaway in the Ford Transit.

Harry put down the album. 'Why does he keep them?' he asked Rebecca, who was now sprawled across the bottom of the bed.

She shrugged. 'I suppose he gets a kick out of it. Or it's something to show his grand-children in his old age.'

'He's got a family back in England, has he?'

'I don't know. He's got a wife, I do know that. Unless she's divorced him by now.' She replaced the album in the bedside cabinet.

'Right. Re-join the crazy gang, shall we?'

'I suppose we'd better.'

She came close to him. 'How long are you on holiday for?'

'Two weeks.'

'Oh well, we've plenty of time yet, then.' And she stood on her tip-toes and gave him another kiss, though this one was more chaste, with closed lips. Then she opened the door and went out, leaving him to follow.

As he expected, Jill had noticed his absence. 'And what were you two up to?' She said it with a smile, even playfully, but she was curious, too.

'Rebecca was showing me some press-cuttings of Norris's,' he said, seeing no reason why the truth shouldn't serve as well as any lie.

'What sort of press-cuttings?'

'Accounts of robberies he's been involved in.'

She stared in surprise. 'He keeps them to read?'

'Yes. I'm sure he'll let you have a look if you ask him.'

'I'm not that interested, thanks.'

He smiled. 'Neither am I. It was just something Rebecca mentioned this afternoon.'

It was a mistake. He knew the moment he'd spoken that it was a mistake but couldn't do much about it except calmly endure the questions that had to follow.

'You saw her this afternoon?'

'Yes.'

'Where?'

'At the marina place. Porto whatever-it's-called.'

'You knew she'd be there?'

'No. I just happened to bump into her.'

'You never told me.'

'No, well, it didn't seem to matter. We just looked at the boats and that was it. Now, do you want another drink or what?'

'Yes, please.'

'Another Perrier water?'

'No. A brandy if there is one.'

When he returned with the brandy and a beer for himself she said, 'She fancies you, you know.'

73

He managed a laugh. 'I doubt it.'

'Yes, she does. I was watching last night.'

'I'm sure she'll get over it,' he said, hoping to keep things light.

He stayed with Jill for the remainder of the evening. It wasn't that he felt the need to placate her; she seemed happy enough with her brandy, chatting to Mats and Kerstin about life in Sweden. But there was no sense in testing her tolerance to its limits.

Rebecca, anyway, seemed to have disappeared. Whether she'd reappear before the end of his holiday remained to be seen. When Jill showed signs of tiring of the party, he suggested they left and she agreed. They went to find Norris, who seemed bemused by drink but insisted on shaking hands with both of them and arranging for Alan Mullins to chauffeur them back. They called goodbye to the roomful of guests, who seemed fewer than earlier. Perhaps others, too, had already slipped away.

'Quiet sort of evening, wasn't it?' said Mullins as he drove. 'Leastways it has been up to now. We'll be having a hand of cards later.'

Harry remembered the row between Fieldhouse and his girl-friend. 'How long will that go on?' he asked.

'Oh, could be all night of a job. I suppose you could join us if you like, but it's men only if you know what I mean.'

'Don't let me stop you,' said Jill with a yawn.

'You're not doing,' said Harry, taking her hand. 'I don't want to, that's all.'

Mullins dropped them off, cursing the narrow road, which meant he'd have to continue as far as the Café Ricco before he could turn. Harry unlocked the gate and they went in.

He half-expected her to return to the subject of Rebecca, but she didn't. Either her suspicions were allayed or she was wiser than to betray them. He helped himself to a night-cap and wandered around the silent villa while Jill undressed. By the time he came to the bedroom she was already asleep. Looking at her, he surprised himself by feeling relief that nothing more had happened that evening.

Neither of them was disturbed by the cavalcade that swept up the road outside some three hours later. It was led by an unmarked police car inside which were four men in uniform. Then came a black Mercedes, with two policemen in a jeep bringing up the rear.

In the back of the Mercedes sat a single, middle-aged man. He was formally dressed in suit and tie, though he was in need of a shave. He stared impassively ahead, ignoring the moonlit scenery through which they were moving.

Ten minutes later the vehicles came to the pink villa which had been the scene of a party and was now the scene of something more serious. The man in the back of the Mercedes waited until the car door was respectfully opened before he climbed out and allowed himself to be led around the side of the villa and into its gardens. An emergency arc-light had been erected to supplement the underwater lights of the swimming-pool. It showed another two policemen already waiting and a civilian holding a doctor's bag. At their feet, by the side of the pool from which he'd been pulled, lay the inert body of a man dressed in white shirt and trousers.

7.

His first reaction to the bell was to reach out in an attempt to silence it before it awakened Jill too, as he did on those mornings when he was making an early start and she was on holiday, wanting a lie-in. But his hand felt only the glass top of the bedside table; there was no alarm clock, and, of course, they weren't at home in Islington but in Spain, in Leo Shapiro's villa.

And the bell meant someone was at the gate.

'What time is it?' protested Jill without opening her eyes.

He looked at his watch. 'Half-seven.'

It rang again, a long, insistent peal that demanded a response.

'Christ.' He pulled himself out of the bed and reached for the nearest clothes to hand, the ones he'd been wearing the night before.

'Who is it?' asked Jill, bewildered.

'I haven't the slightest idea.'

She groaned and pulled the bedclothes over her head. Harry stepped into his shoes, grabbed the bunch of keys and hurried out.

It was Rebecca beyond the wrought ironwork. Even as his spirits leapt at the sight of her, he saw her face and knew something was wrong. Her expression was set, and she stood without a move of recognition or greeting as he came and unlocked the gate.

'Something's happened,' she said.

'What? Are you all right?'

'I'm all right,' she said, coming in past him. 'Norris is dead.'

'What?' It wasn't that he hadn't heard; just that such a statement could be met only by disbelief.

'He's dead. They found him in the swimming-pool early this

morning. The police are there.'

He nodded to show he understood but could think of little to say. The death of Norris, whose villainy was well-documented, could hardly be a signal for national, or even local, mourning. Even Rebecca, his mistress, hadn't seemed to like him much. Now she appeared stunned, perhaps as unsure of her own reactions as Harry was of his.

He took her elbow and steered her into the kitchen.

'Sit down. You want some coffee?'

'I wouldn't mind a glass of water. I've been drinking coffee all night.'

Jill came in from the bedroom, drawn by the sound of voices. She was fastening the buttons of a beach-robe that reached to her knees. Taking in the scene, she looked from Rebecca to Harry.

'Norris is dead,' said Harry, using Rebecca's phrase as the only one he could rely on, since the circumstances of his death were still a mystery.

Jill let a moment pass, then said simply, 'How?'

'Drowned,' said Rebecca, then gave a shrug as though to dissociate herself from the diagnosis. 'They found him in the swimming-pool. They said he was drunk. And probably stoned as well.'

'I see,' said Jill. 'And when was this?'

'About three o'clock.'

'And you found him, did you?'

'No. Oh no, I wasn't even there. Alan and Gerald, they found him.'

'And then they phoned you?' said Harry, trying to assemble the pieces.

'Eventually, yes. I mean first they phoned a doctor. Then he had to notify the police, so they were all over the place. And because they decided it was a suspicious death they sent for the local . . . ' She hesitated. 'Well, I don't know what you'd call him. In Spanish it's *juez de guardia*. A sort of a prosecutor.'

'Magistrate . . . ?' offered Jill.

'Well, more powerful than that. Where there are suspicious

77

circumstances he has to see the body before it's moved and then he decides whether the police should investigate or whatever. Anyway, he was called.'

'I'll make us some coffee,' muttered Jill, and she began to move quietly about the kitchen.

'And what does he think?' asked Harry.

'Who?'

'This magistrate or whatever he is.'

'I don't know. He's already talked to Alan and Gerald and he wants to see me later this morning. He might want to see you since you were at the party. That's why I thought I'd better let you know. Well, that and I thought you'd want to know anyway.'

'Of course,' said Harry. 'And we're sorry. It must have been . . . been a great shock.' It would have been easier to offer consolation had he not heard her slagging Norris off while she haunted the marina of Porto Banus on the look-out for a new boy-friend.

She gave a wry smile. 'It was a bit.'

'I'll make us some toast,' said Jill. 'Then anybody who wants any can help themselves.'

'But are they regarding it as an accident?' asked Harry, still unclear as to just what sort of police enquiry was under way.

'Probably. They'll view it as whatever they like. I don't think they could care less one way or the other. Probably be delighted if we all killed one another off, then they'd be spared the bother of extradition treaties and the like.'

Harry felt bound to protest: 'But with Norris being who he was . . . ? I mean, won't that force them to make some sort of effort?'

'No.' She spoke quietly but without any doubt.

'Oh.'

'That's precisely *why* they won't.'

'But is there really any doubt it was an accident?' asked Jill.

There was a pause as Rebecca stared into her glass of water, then she shrugged and said, 'I don't know.'

'So you do have doubts?' persisted Jill.

'Me?' Another hesitation, then: 'Yes, I suppose I do.'

'Why?'

'Oh, lots of things. But nothing very specific. No actual evidence if that's what you mean.'

There was something odd about this post-mortem being held in the sun-filled kitchen while the coffee percolated and the toaster produced two slices of medium-brown toast. We're none of us expressing sympathy for Norris, realised Harry. The only shared reaction was surprise and curiosity as to what might happen next.

Rebecca went on: 'There was something peculiar about the way he was behaving last night. All that drinking . . . he didn't normally drink like that.'

Harry remembered Norris waving his bottle of vodka. 'Perhaps he didn't feel the party was going very well . . . ?'

'That's another thing.'

'What?'

'I don't know why he wanted the bloody party in the first place. And those people he invited. I mean they were neighbours mostly, not the sort of crowd he usually mixed with.'

'No?'

'He didn't even like parties,' she said, and fell silent.

'Is there, er . . . is there anything we can do?'

'Yes,' murmured Jill in support.

'Not really. Thanks all the same. I'm just sorry you've been involved. But we had to give the police a list of who was at the party.'

'Who actually found him?' asked Harry.

'I think it was both Alan and Gerald together. They were the only two still there.' She stood up. 'Anyway, I'd better go.'

They urged her to stay and have some breakfast or perhaps even use one of the beds in the villa to catch up on the rest she so clearly needed, but she was adamant about leaving. Harry walked her to the gate.

'I suppose you think I'm being stupid,' she said. 'I mean not accepting it's like they're saying. That he got pissed and fell in.'

'It's early days,' said Harry. 'I'm sure they'll find out what happened one way or another.'

She gave him a look that was almost pitying. 'No, they won't,' she said firmly. 'Why should they? Norris was somebody they could well have done without, and now they've got rid of him without having to bother the courts. It's a God-send.'

'It might be. But then some accidents are. It doesn't mean somebody has to have murdered him.'

She stiffened at his use of the word 'murder', as though by doing so he'd broken a taboo and become her ally.

'Suppose somebody did, though? Will you help me find out?'

'Me . . . ?'

'Please.'

It was crazy to think he might start playing detective on foreign soil. Why should he care anyway how Norris Edgerton met his fate? The man had been a shotgun-waving villain, inflicting violence on others when it suited him. If he'd been bumped off then it was no more than he'd deserved. A firm no was the only sensible answer to her plea for help; but, fancying her as he did, sense hardly came into it.

'You're upset,' he said.

'I am not upset.' Her old confidence asserted itself through the tiredness and the shock. 'Well, not in the way you mean. You mean I'm too emotional to think straight. Well, I'm not that.'

'No, all right. But perhaps none of us can think straight. It's too soon. Wait.'

'I'll pay you.'

'Oh, come on,' he protested.

'Why not? You're a private detective. OK, I'll pay you to work for me.'

'You don't have to pay me. All I'm saying is wait. See what the autopsy says. See what the police come up with. Then see whether you still feel like you do now.'

'The police will come up with nothing. The autopsy will say he drowned. And yes, I will still feel like I do now.'

'Well, then . . . ' He hesitated, knowing it was foolish to give

80

any sort of commitment but knowing, too, that it would be mutual, bringing them together, even if it were in futile pursuit. 'Then we'll talk about it.'

'You promise?'

'Yes.'

She smiled and then, as she moved away to her car, called, 'I'll be at the café tonight. See you there, OK?'

'If I can.'

'You will.'

She was a merciless and outrageous flirt, even when calling to announce the death of her lover. It was that he found most attractive.

They spent the day on the beach. Excursions to look at monasteries or bull-rings seemed out of the question with Norris's untimely death dominating their thoughts and conversation. They lay in what was becoming their regular spot, making occasional forays to the ramshackle restaurant for food and drink and pausing en route to see what the sand-sculptor was up to. They each had a book but neither read much, preferring to doze or offer yet another observation on Rebecca's visit that morning.

'I thought she lived with him,' said Jill.

'Only part-time I think,' said Harry. 'You remember she said she had a flat in Marbella . . . ?' Wanting to remind her that this was shared information, not something bestowed on him alone at some secret meeting.

'Yes, but you'd think she'd have stayed with Norris after the party. Since she was there already.'

He had to agree. 'I suppose so. Except that they were planning on playing cards for the rest of the night.'

'That didn't mean she had to be off the premises, surely . . . !'

'No. Oh, I don't know. Perhaps that was the way she preferred it.'

A gypsy woman came and stood above them, displaying lace tablecloths. They told her no thank you, but she persevered until they were forced to turn their backs and ignore her.

'He was pretty drunk,' mused Jill.

'Well oiled,' Harry agreed.

'And if he was taking drugs as well . . . '

'It wouldn't be all that difficult for him to end up in his own swimming-pool.'

'No.'

A family arrived and established themselves close by, unpacking chairs, packets of food and a small Primus stove.

'And, of course,' said Jill slowly, 'there was Tommy Smith.'

'Yes.'

'You remember? The one they said had disappeared.'

'I remember, yes.' In fact, he'd thought of Tommy Smith, the fourth drinking crony of Leo Shapiro, even while Rebecca had been telling them her dreadful news.

'So can it be just coincidence?' wondered Jill. 'He disappears, and then a few weeks later this happens.'

'It could be, yes.'

'Do you think it is? Honestly?'

'I honestly don't know.'

By mid-afternoon they had had enough of the sun and started on a gentle stroll back to the villa. An underpass dipped beneath the roadway, then brought them out in front of the Café Ricco.

Harry nodded towards it. 'Rebecca said she'd be in there tonight.'

Jill looked in surprise. 'Drowning her sorrows?'

'I don't know. But I got the impression she'd welcome some company if we weren't doing anything else.'

'And are we?'

'I don't know.'

Jill said nothing and they continued up the increasingly familiar road. Once inside the villa, Harry elected to go for a swim – their own pool was dazzling with sunlight and didn't seem to threaten any of the dangers Norris had found in his – while Jill went for a shower. He was completing his third length when the telephone began to ring. He hauled himself out and,

82

with no towel within reach, went dripping through the lounge and lifted the receiver.

'Hello?'

A man answered, cheerful and English, though it wasn't a voice Harry could identify.

'Mr Sommers?'

'Yes.'

'I'm ringing on behalf of the *juez de guardia* here. My name's Robert Devine, and I'm acting as interpreter for them. It's about the death of Norris Edgerton. You know about that, do you?'

'Yes. Heard about it this morning.'

'Yes, well, it's no more than a formality really, but they want to talk to some of the people who saw him last, and your name's been given as someone who was at this party he gave. You were there, weren't you?'

'Yes, but not . . . I mean he was all right when we left.'

'Oh, I'm sure he was. But the judge would like to hear that from your own lips if you can spare us ten minutes.'

'Well, yes, I suppose . . . why not?' It sounded in any case like the kind of courteous request that would quickly turn into an abrupt command should he refuse to comply.

'Terrific. Do you have a car?'

Harry said he had, at which Robert Devine said, 'Terrific,' again and then set about giving him directions as to how to find the police-station from which the judge was conducting his investigation.

'See you in about twenty minutes, then,' he said when they'd got everything clear.

'OK,' said Harry, and rang off. He went to find Jill in the bathroom, where she was still beneath the shower.

'Don't do that!' she said, startled by his entry.

'I've got to go and talk to this judge character.' He told her about his summons while finding a towel to dry himself.

'And so what are you going to tell them?' she said, concerned.

He shrugged. 'Not a lot. There isn't much I can tell them, is there?'

83

'Don't they want to see me?'

'Doesn't sound like it. I imagine they just want to speak to a sample of the people who were there, and my name happened to come out of the hat.'

'Be careful, won't you?'

'What of?'

'I don't know. That's why I think you should be careful.'

The police-station was in a small town, twelve kilometres away, a place to which tourists would come only by accident or out of necessity. Arriving in the whitewashed square that formed its centre, Harry was conscious that here was another Spain, ancient and private. There was a squat church with a bell suspended above it and, to the side of the door, a crucifix on which a life-sized Christ bled vividly. The police-station was to its right, its windows shuttered and its huge oak door studded like that of any fortress. It stood ajar, and from it, as Harry approached, came a thin young man with a ginger beard and khaki shorts.

'Mr Sommers?'

'Yes.'

'I'm Robert Devine.' They shook hands. 'I work as a teacher here in the town. It's just occasionally, when they need an interpreter, they ask me to come in. It's normally when someone's reported a robbery. I've never had anything like this to deal with before.'

He led Harry into the cool darkness of the building where three green-uniformed policemen were sat at their ease, smoking and drinking coffee. There was a picture of King Carlos on the wall and another of the Blessed Virgin with a votive light beneath it. Below that was a row of guns, each in its holster and hanging from a numbered wooden peg.

Harry followed Robert Devine past the dispassionate stares of the policemen and up a wooden staircase, the treads of which had been worn away until they bowed in the middle.

'Here we are,' said Devine when they reached the door at the top. 'Now don't worry. This is all very informal.'

Harry, who was highly intrigued and not in the least bit worried, followed him into a long room where the shutters had been opened to admit some sunlight. A middle-aged man in a suit and tie sat at the head of a pitted table. Although now clean-shaven save for a finely trimmed moustache, he had about him an air of weariness and managed no more than a grunt and a nod towards the entering pair.

'Sit down,' whispered Devine, placing himself on a chair at the side of the table and indicating another one beside it.

Harry sat down and cleared his throat. There was a silence; then the whine of a motorcycle came into the square below the windows before receding into the distance. The judge, who had been examining his fingernails, spoke in a low monotone without looking at either of them.

'¿Cómo se llama usted, y cuál es su nacionalidad?'

'Would you please state your name and nationality,' translated Devine.

Not sure which of them to address, Harry aimed his answer at the air between them. 'Harry Sommers. British.'

'Enrique Sommers. Británica,' translated Devine.

The judge showed no sign of having heard, then removed a fountain-pen from the inside pocket of his jacket, unscrewed the top, turned to Devine and gave a small jerk of his head.

'Enrique Sommers. Británica,' Devine repeated.

The judge took his fountain-pen and wrote in an ornate, italic hand in the ledger that was open before him. Only when he had completed this did he speak again.

'¿Profesión?'

'Occupation?' said Devine.

'Private detective,' said Harry.

Devine looked at him in surprise and waited a moment, as though expecting Harry to admit he was joking. When he didn't, he turned to the judge and said, 'Detective privado.'

The judge showed not a flicker of either interest or doubt but wrote carefully in his ledger.

'¿Qué parentesco había entre usted y el difunto?'

85

Devine turned to Harry: 'What was your relationship to the deceased?'

'Well, I met him the day after I'd arrived here. He was a friend of the man whose villa we're staying in. And then he invited us to the party. So that was only really the second time I'd met him.'

As Devine patiently translated, the judge seemed to lose interest and went back to contemplating his fingernails. Then he spoke, briefly and dismissively.

'¿Se puede decir que eran amigos?'

'Can he say you were friends?'

'Yes.'

'Sí. Eran amigos.'

'Amigos,' sighed the judge, and wrote in his ledger.

There was something soothing, even soporific, about the form of the interrogation. The judge would speak, never varying his low monotone nor seeming able to rouse himself from his state of boredom. Devine would translate in an eager whisper, Harry reply, Devine again, then out would come the fountain-pen, and the room would fall silent while Harry's reply was painstakingly recorded.

'¿Cuándo habló por última vez con el señor Edgerton, el difunto?'

'When did you last speak to Norris Edgerton, the deceased?'

'At the party. Last night.'

'En la fiesta. Anoche,' said Devine.

'¿Qué impresión le causó su estado de ánimo?'

'What was your impression of his state of mind?'

'Well, he seemed . . . he seemed to be all right really.'

'Me pareció bien.'

'¿Habiá estado bebiendo?'

'Had he been drinking?'

'Yes.'

'Sí.'

'¿Mucho?'

'A lot?'

Harry hesitated, then said, 'A fair amount, yes.'

'Bastante, sí.'

'¿Le indicó algo a usted que él había estado pensando en suicidarse?'

'Did he say anything to you that indicated he might have been thinking of taking his own life?'

The question surprised Harry. It was an option none of them, not even Rebecca, had considered.

'No. Oh no, definitely not.'

The judge this time began to write without needing to wait for Devine's translation.

'No. En absoluto.'

'¿Parecía temer por su vida?'

'Did he seem in fear for his life?'

Harry considered. 'No,' he said. He thought back to Norris urging his guests to eat, drink and listen to Manitas de Plata and remembered his forthright exchange with Heinz, the retired Munich lawyer, about the legal profession and their similarity to birds of prey, and then the befuddled but hardly fearful state he'd been in when they left. 'No,' he repeated with conviction. 'Not at all.'

'No,' said Devine. 'De ninguna manera.'

'¿Tiene alguna información referente a la muerte del señor Edgerton?'

'Have you any information regarding Mr Edgerton which may be relevant to his death?'

Did that mean apart from the fact he had a criminal record as long as your arm and was on the run from the forces of law and order in his own country? Should he mention the album of press-cuttings detailing his most recent exploits? And what about Tommy Smith, erstwhile friend and colleague, now mysteriously missing?

'No,' said Harry. 'None.'

'No. Ninguna.'

The judge nodded, then said, 'Gratias.'

'That's it,' said Devine. 'You can go.'

Harry came out into the square. He knew now, suddenly, that Rebecca had been right. Not perhaps in suspecting there was more to Norris's death than it appeared. That remained to be seen. But she'd surely been right in claiming that the Spanish authorities weren't interested.

They were going through the motions, and doing so in a leisurely, rather stately fashion. Conducting a few slow-motion interviews for a file that could then safely be closed and locked away. The death of Norris Edgerton was an accident and was going to stay that way.

'I'm sure we won't be troubling you again,' said Devine brightly, shaking hands. 'So you can enjoy the rest of your holiday.'

'Cheers,' said Harry, and walked to where he'd parked the Seat.

Hadn't he himself become an accomplice to the cover-up when he'd answered the final question? '¿Tiene alguna información referente a la muerte del señor Edgerton?' 'No,' he'd replied. 'None.' Which, when you thought about it, was a lie.

The judge may well have known this. The judge may well have known a great deal but was probably relieved that Harry had lied and so hadn't complicated things. But then the judge had to answer only to his superiors and his own conscience, not to Rebecca.

Harry got back to find Jill changed for the evening, looking cool and relaxed.

'What happened?'

'Not a lot. I was asked about how long I'd known Norris and what he'd been like at the party.'

'Drunk.'

'Well, yes. And that was about it.'

'They didn't ask you about what he'd got up to in England?'

'No. They didn't seem very interested. I'm sure they'll be happy to call it an accident and leave it at that.'

'You didn't mention my handbag?'

'What?' he said in surprise.

'That business when those boys grabbed my handbag. I was thinking about it after you went. I mean they were rather badly beaten up. It couldn't have been some sort of revenge attack by them, could it?'

It was a new angle, in a situation that already had too many for comfort.

'I shouldn't think so,' said Harry. 'But, anyway, I didn't mention it, no.'

They ate out at a restaurant in Marbella where fish was charcoaled over an open barbecue. Neither was inclined to raise again the topic of Norris's death till, returning past the Café Ricco, they spotted Rebecca at a table with Mullins, Fieldhouse and Samantha.

'The gang are still gathering, then,' Jill commented.

'It looks like it.'

'You go and join them if you like. I'm feeling whacked.'

He shot her a sideways glance. 'You're sure?'

She yawned. 'Yes. It's you Rebecca wants to see anyway.'

She spoke calmly, so he took her at her word and said he'd pop down for a drink but wouldn't be too late and would make sure she was safely locked up in the villa during his absence. She nodded, happy enough, or perhaps simply indifferent. Certainly the last few days, which had seen her thrown headlong into the company of villains, having her handbag snatched and then attending a party where the host had ended up dead in his own swimming-pool, seemed to have broken her long-standing resolve to keep him away from his former, criminal acquaintances.

'Good night,' he said, and kissed her.

'Good night, Harry. Be careful.'

8.

She was waiting at the café when he arrived, attracting lustful glances and working her way through a bottle of white wine. She appeared rested, recovered from the shock. The rest of the gang, as Jill had termed them, had disappeared.

'So,' he said, 'how do you feel now? You still think there was something suspicious about what happened?'

'Yes,' she said, looking him in the eye. 'I do.'

'I was afraid you might.'

She smiled, then said, 'Have the police been to see you?'

'I was summonsed to see them. Or at least to see that judge or whatever he is.'

'What did he want to know?'

'Not a lot. Just wanted me to agree with him that Norris had died by accident.'

She smiled again, vindicated. 'So now you see what I mean. There isn't going to be any big investigation.'

'Possibly not. But that doesn't mean we have to attempt one.'

'It might be fun.' She spoke lightly, as though the whole thing were a game. 'And, anyway, I thought you detectives were driven by a passion for justice . . . ?'

'I'm on holiday.' Then quickly, before she could protest: 'But seriously . . . ' Seeing she was still smiling, he insisted: 'Seriously.' Her smile disappeared. 'Why bother? Why pursue this if the police won't?'

'I could say it was out of love for Norris.'

'You could.'

'But you wouldn't believe me if I did.' He held her gaze and said nothing. 'All right, it's not out of love for Norris. Because there was never much of that at the best of times. But I want to know. I want to know what really happened. Don't you?'

He hesitated, then admitted, 'I'm curious.'

'Curious,' she echoed wryly. 'Yes, well, call it that if you like. I'm curious, too. I'm bloody curious.'

She made it sound a powerful motive. She was, he recognised, one of life's gypsies, letting fate take her where it would, then exploring the emotional landscape wherever it set her down. She'd first started sleeping with Norris in order to understand his criminality. Now she wanted to know who'd killed him and why.

'I'll get some more wine,' said Harry. He caught the eye of Luigi, Mullins's boy-friend, who came and took their order with an exaggerated solemnity, imagining them to be in mourning.

'So tell me,' resumed Harry when he'd gone, 'what makes you think Norris was murdered?'

He didn't have to ask twice. She'd obviously assembled her theories and was now eager to advance them. 'Well, point one – Tommy Smith.'

'Ah.'

'I told you about Tommy, right? How he just disappeared. I know Norris always believed there was something wrong about that. That he'd been murdered or abducted or something. Well, now Norris has gone as well.'

'OK.'

'Point two. Norris didn't normally drink. He was careful about keeping fit, looking after himself.'

'He looked to be putting it away last night.'

'But why? That's what I'm saying. There was something going on that made him act like that. And then he as good as kicked me out of the house!'

'What house?'

'His villa. I was going to stay. I don't mean necessarily sleep with him but just stay there. Till he made it abundantly clear he wanted me out. So I said sod you. And went.'

Luigi returned with a bottle of wine which he ceremoniously opened and placed on the table before them.

'They were going to have a game of cards,' said Harry.

'That didn't mean everybody had to be off the premises. I could have gone to bed, for Christ's sake. And, anyway, it wasn't just that. He'd been acting strangely for a week or two.'

'How?'

'Oh, as though something was worrying him. Something he didn't want me to know about.'

Harry topped up both their glasses, then said, 'Do you think Fieldhouse and Mullins killed him?'

For the first time he caught her off guard. 'Oh no. No, I'm not saying that.'

'Why not? They were the only two left there with him.'

She shook her head. 'I just . . . no, I don't think so.'

'Why not?' he insisted.

'Oh, I don't know. I just can't see them working together. Gerald thinks Alan is a pathetic little queer, and Alan regards Gerald as some sort of homicidal maniac.'

'And is he?'

'Probably, yes.'

'So perhaps Gerald killed Norris on his own?'

But she was still reluctant. 'Well, I can't see . . . I mean Norris was the one who made all the decisions. He'd re-cruited them for the Bond Street raid and then, when they were over here, he was always the boss, the one who gave the orders.'

Harry was reminded of the album of press-cuttings testifying to Norris's criminal past. Did it also contain the key to understanding his murder? Had his death been a settling of old scores from way back over the water, rivalries or unpaid debts established in the damp atmosphere of London's streets rather than in the warmth of Spain?

'Did he have any enemies? People who might one day catch up with him?'

She gave it serious thought. 'Only the police.'

'The police . . . ?'

'The English police.'

Well, yes. They had had their marker out on Norris for some time. But it was one that surely lay with the courts and the British embassy in Madrid, not with some contract hit-man operating on tax-payers' money.

She put her hand over his. 'Harry, you'll help me, won't you?'

'I don't know what I can do,' he said in token protest.

'You can talk to Alan, talk to Gerald. . . . Well, you're the detective. Do whatever you'd do if it had happened in England.'

If it had happened in England, he'd have dialled 999 and backed away sharpish.

'I'll talk to them. But I'm not promising anything.'

'I love it when you're corny.'

'What?'

'I'm not promising anything,' she mimicked him. 'Don't you private eyes always say that?'

'Sometimes we mean it. I can talk to Mullins and Fieldhouse. Oh, and perhaps to the doctor who was called, if we can find out who he is. As far as I can see, that's about it.'

But she wasn't to be put off. Just smiled and said, 'Don't forget you'll have me helping.'

Well, no, he wouldn't forget that since it was the sole reason for his being involved at all. She was beautiful and provocative, and her cry for help was irresistible.

She was also suddenly tired and was asking Luigi to arrange a taxi for her. Harry saw it had gone one o'clock. They made a vague arrangement to meet again and then, with a quick kiss, she was gone, leaving him to walk back to the villa where Jill was sleeping.

Alan Mullins presented himself ready and willing to be interviewed at nine-thirty the following morning while Harry and Jill were still having breakfast and planning the day's campaign.

'Sorry if I'm a bit early,' he said. 'But Rebecca said you wanted to see me and it's sort of urgent.'

'Well, not all that urgent,' said Harry, aware of Jill's gaze. 'But I wouldn't mind a word, yes.'

'I'll leave you to it, shall I?' said Jill, picking up her cup and plate.

93

Harry ignored the trace of sarcasm. 'We won't be long,' he promised.

'Take all the time in the world,' she said, and went out.

'Hope I'm not upsetting things,' said Mullins.

'She'll get over it,' said Harry, then noticed the door was ajar and hurried to close it. 'Would you like a coffee?'

'No, thanks all the same. Gives me palpitations, too much coffee this time of a morning.'

'Did Rebecca tell you that, er . . . ' He hesitated, not sure how to describe the role he'd taken on, but Mullins was already nodding eagerly.

'You're doing some poking around, like. See if there was any more to poor old Norris's death than meets the eye.'

'Something like that.'

'Well, we want to know, don't we? And the Spaniards aren't going to tell us. He could have had a knife sticking out of his back and they'd still call it an accident. No, you fire away, old son.'

Encouraged, Harry said, 'Well, just tell me what happened. Say, from the time I left the party. What happened after that?'

'Oh well, let's see. You left . . . and then other people left . . . till there was only me, Gerald and Norris. I mean I know for sure there was nobody else because one of the things I was doing, I went round the whole place collecting glasses and plates and anything else that had been left about. In the garden, everywhere. So if anybody had been around I would have seen 'em.'

'Was the gate locked?'

Mullins thought about it, then said, 'No. No, because when we phoned for the doctor and he arrived . . . No, it wasn't.'

'OK. So, anyway, everybody had left . . . ?'

'Yes. See, we was going to play cards. Planning on making a night of it. Only first of all we had to clear away some of the crap that had been left everywhere on account of it was like a tap-room at closing-time and we needed the table. So me and Gerald starts doing this, and Norris says he's going out for some fresh air. Which he needed.'

'What sort of state was he in?'

'Somewhere between pissed and extremely pissed.'

'Was that usual?'

'No. Oh, I don't mean to say it'd never happened before. He'd go on a bender from time to time, would old Norris, just like anybody else. But it wasn't what you'd call a regular occurrence.'

'So what was special about last night?'

'Nothing I know of. He just started drinking early, that's all. I mean you do sometimes, don't you?'

'So he went outside . . . ?' prompted Harry.

'He went outside while we cleared the crap. Which didn't make Gerald very happy, but then Gerald isn't what you'd call your domestic type. And then we was ready to start. But still no Norris. So we have a drink, shuffle the cards, wait a bit . . . still no Norris. So we both go outside to have a look.'

'Together?'

'Every step of the way. Not that we thought anything nasty had happened. Just that we'd both been waiting, then we both went out to look for him and . . . there he was.'

'In the pool?'

Mullins nodded. 'Floating. Face down and floating. I mean as soon as we saw him . . . well, it was obvious.'

'So what did you do?'

'Oh, we pulled him out. Which wasn't easy, him being a big feller and that, but we managed it between us. We thought about the kiss-of-life and all that like they tell you, but . . . well, he was dead. No pulse, no nothing.'

'Did you hear anything?'

'When?'

'When Norris was outside. Before you found him.'

'No. Nothing.'

'And then you phoned for a doctor?'

'Yes. And then he had to let the police know, and the body couldn't be moved until this judge had been and seen it. All of a sudden it was like the circus was in town.'

'Right.' There was a moment of respectful silence, then Harry asked, 'What do you think, Alan?'

'Me?'

'Yes. Was it an accident or was Norris helped into that pool?'

Mullins took time to consider, then slowly shook his head. 'I don't know, Harry. I really and truly don't know.'

'Was he on anything else besides the booze?'

Mullins shrugged and looked doubtful. 'He might have smoked the odd joint but not the heavy stuff. Not as I was aware.'

'Was he involved in any kind of racket over here? Smuggling, handling . . . anything?'

The same reaction. 'If he was, then I knew nothing about it. See, it wasn't worth the candle. Not over here. The slightest thing and they'd have you out, no messing. Straight back to Blighty with two gentlemen from Scotland Yard waiting for you as you got off the plane.'

'How was he for money?'

'Norris? Oh, comfortable. No problems in that direction. He was well set up, was Norris.'

'And who'll get it now?'

'Well . . . his wife I suppose. They're the ones that usually benefit, aren't they?'

'Where does she live?'

'Around London somewhere. I don't know exactly.'

'Has anybody told her yet?'

'Don't know. Not me, I can promise you that.'

'Rebecca reckons Norris had changed over the last few weeks. Something about his manner or his attitude that was different.'

Mullins was unimpressed by the suggestion. 'Not as I was aware.' Then he added, conspiratorially: ''Course, if he was getting tired of her and was planning on giving her the elbow, then perhaps his attitude did change, but only towards her if you see what I mean.'

Harry did. 'And was he planning on giving her the elbow?'

'Oh, I wouldn't know. Last thing old Norris would talk to me about, is that.'

Running out of questions, Harry tried his only remaining

angle. 'Did you work with Norris back in England?'

Mullins squirmed, as though fearful of incriminating himself, then admitted, 'Once or twice, yes.'

'On that jeweller's job he did in Bond Street?'

Another hesitation, then: 'I might have done.'

'What about Gerald? Was he in on that?'

But now the defences were up. 'You'll have to ask him. I can only speak for myself and nobody else.'

'What about Tommy Smith?'

'Tommy . . . ?'

'Did he ever work with Norris at all?'

Mullins relaxed. 'Might have done. They went back a long way, did Norris and Tommy. Further than Norris and me, so I can't tell you. Sorry.'

They left it at that. Mullins departed, assuring Harry that if there was anything else he could do then Harry had only to ask and calling, 'Bye, love', through to Jill, who was sitting out on the patio.

'So what was that all about?' she said as he joined her. 'Or am I not supposed to know?'

'I promised Rebecca I'd help her tie up one or two loose ends where Norris was concerned.'

'You're working for her?'

'Not exactly.'

'You're working for her, but she's not paying you?'

'Something like that,' he admitted.

She looked at him and shook her head. 'God, Harry . . . ' she said quietly.

'I know. I know. But it won't spoil the holiday, I promise it won't.'

She tried to hide her smile but couldn't. 'I'm sure it won't. After everything that's happened already anything else will be an anti-climax. You do your investigating or whatever else makes you happy. But just leave me out of it, OK?'

'Of course.'

'I'll stick to sight-seeing and sunbathing for my kicks.'

They decided to visit Gibraltar and hurried to leave so as to arrive before lunch. The Rock, rising from the sea, was as spectacular as either could have wished, but, crossing on to it, they found themselves in a strange world that was an amalgam of army town, naval base and tourist centre, scruffy and crowded, a foreign territory for which they needed their passports and were suddenly back to English money. They took the cable-car up the mountain-side and saw the odd monkey playing with itself and posing for photographs. There was an aircraft-carrier in the harbour and, in the open seas beyond, a flotilla of small- and medium-sized boats moving slowly about their business.

It was a perspective on to a larger world. Was it also one in which both Norris Edgerton and Tommy Smith had moved and in which both had come unstuck? Harry kept such thoughts to himself and followed Jill as she perused the shops and speculated about how long Britain could sustain such remnants of Empire. Harry saw the Union Jacks and the bunting and could think only of London, where such decoration would signal hostility to its ethnic minorities.

By early evening they had had their fill of sight-seeing and dined in a restaurant called the Fox and Hounds. Then they re-crossed the boundary with its small customs-post and came back into Spain, oddly relieved to leave the huddled streets that seemed more like a poor representation of English life, dated and tawdry, than the real thing.

Harry drove. As they passed through Estepona, he asked Jill whether she wanted to return to the villa or stop off somewhere for a drink.

'It's up to you,' she said.

'I don't mind.'

'What about your investigation? Aren't you still pursuing that?' It was a topic neither had raised while on British sovereign territory. Clearly the return to Spain had placed it back on the agenda.

'I told you it wouldn't interfere with our holiday,' he said carefully. 'And it won't.'

'No. Sorry,' she said, sounding suddenly downcast. 'Actually

I would rather get back if you don't mind. I feel filthy. And pretty tired as well.'

'The villa it is, then.'

In the ten minutes it took them to reach their turn-off by the Café Ricco, the evening had nose-dived into darkness.

'I feel like a swim,' announced Harry as they entered their front door, switching on lights and dropping their bags on to the marble floor.

'You won't be able to see,' she objected mildly.

'I can see enough.' He recalled his earlier dreams of nude-bathing and wondered if this was the moment. 'Why don't you join me?'

'No, thanks. I need a hot bath.'

Evidently it wasn't the moment. Perhaps there wouldn't be one. She went towards the bathroom while he switched on the patio lights and let himself into the garden. He stepped out of his clothes and flung himself into the dark pool. Deciding to make it an athletic session, since it certainly wasn't going to be an erotic one, he set himself to do twenty lengths without stopping.

Two hours later he emerged from the villa and carefully locked the gate behind him as he'd promised Jill he would when she had announced her intention to make an early night of it. Perhaps she'd sensed his eagerness to be away or perhaps she was simply exhausted by the nights of partying and days spent in the sun.

At first it looked like a replay of the previous evening. Rebecca was already at the Café Ricco, sitting alone and looking stunning in her 'Hertz Rent-A-Car' tee-shirt. As Harry approached, she raised a glass of white wine and said, '*Ciao*.'

'How are you?' he said, sitting across from her.

'Fine,' she said, and leant forward. He realised she expected him to kiss her and did so willingly. 'Have some of this,' she said, pouring some wine into a second glass, 'and tell me what you've been doing today. Did Alan come to see you?'

He nodded. 'First thing this morning.'

'Good. Did he tell you anything interesting?'

'Not really, no.' Except for his suggestion that Norris might have been preparing to give Rebecca the elbow, but there seemed little point in mentioning that.

'And so what else have you been doing today?'

'We went to Gibraltar.'

'That shit-heap!' she exclaimed.

He laughed. 'You don't like it?'

'I loathe it. It's worse than England. In fact, it's worse than anywhere I can think of.'

'Oh, come on,' he said, feeling bound to protest. 'Just what's so wrong with it?'

'If you've really spent a day there you don't need me to tell you.'

He could only wonder at her vehemence. Was Gibraltar's crime that it reminded her of home, a piece of British rock stuck absurdly between Spain and North Africa?

'Finish your glass,' she ordered. 'And then I thought we might go for a little ride.'

'Where to?'

'I'm not telling you. It's a mystery tour.'

She left the table, giving him no option but to follow. He climbed into the passenger side of her Seat and said nothing as they headed past Leo Shapiro's villa – where Jill, hopefully, was now asleep – and then turned sharp right, taking him into an area of half-hearted development he hadn't previously encountered. There were villas without roofs, some with only three walls and others that had yet to rise above their foundations.

'Where the hell are we going?' he asked at last.

'You'll find out in a minute.'

They came to a clump of completed villas with their full complement of walls and roofs. Rebecca slowed and then stopped, coming almost bumper-to-bumper with a white Mercedes.

'First stop on the tour,' she said. 'That's where Tommy Smith lived. And that was his car.'

Harry peered out but couldn't see much in the dark. It seemed to be a villa after the style of the majority: low, white-painted and – of this at least he could be certain – enclosed by the usual barrier of ornate wrought ironwork. The white Mercedes was similarly indistinguishable from so many others on the coast.

'And just what am I supposed to do?' asked Harry.

'Nothing,' she said, re-starting the car, reversing and then pulling out to pass the parked Merc. 'I just thought you might like to see it, that's all.'

They drove for another ten minutes until Harry was surprised to find the route becoming familiar.

'Norris's villa . . . ?' he said.

'You've guessed it. Only this time we can go in.'

'We can?'

'I've still got my keys.'

The pink villa where Norris had lived and then, two nights ago, had died was locked and shuttered with no remnants of a police presence or anything else to hint at what had happened there. They parked before the gates, which Rebecca unlocked. Harry felt a shiver of anticipation as they entered side by side, though whether this was at the prospect of viewing the scene-of-crime or of being alone with Rebecca he couldn't have said.

There had been a perfunctory attempt at tidying up after the party – presumably by Mullins and Fieldhouse in preparation for the intended card school. However, there were still enough unwashed glasses and piled ashtrays about for the place to reek. And small mounds of left-over food beginning to go mouldy.

'Christ,' said Rebecca, wrinkling up her nose. 'The place stinks.'

'Don't tell me we've come here to do the washing-up.'

'No, we haven't. I'll get Francesca to come in and do that. We're here so you can do your detecting.'

'And just what am I supposed to be looking for?'

'Clues.'

He nodded solemnly. 'I see.'

'I'll open some of these windows.'

101

Harry borrowed a torch and wandered out into the garden, unsure that he'd recognise a clue under these circumstances if it jumped up and bit him on the nose. Nevertheless, the lady demanded at least a show of activity, so he began by tracing the perimeter fence and checking that it hadn't been breeched at any point. It was a tricky job in the dark, leading him through thickets and across flower-beds. He made the full circuit, discovering no evidence of intruders. The fence, with its barbed-wire crown, was intact.

'Can you switch the pool lights on?' he called, hoping Rebecca was within earshot. For a few moments he thought she wasn't; then the round underwater lights flickered into life.

Apart from some leaves collecting on the surface, the pool was as he'd remembered it from the party. Nothing to show where Norris had fallen in or been hauled out. Harry walked around it twice for form's sake, then shouted, 'You can turn 'em off now', and returned indoors.

'The police have searched this place I suppose,' he said.

'I wouldn't bank on it,' said Rebecca. 'I would think they'd be frightened of finding anything.' She was wandering around with a carrier-bag, collecting items – kitchen utensils and bric-à-brac – which Harry assumed must have been hers. Either that or she was engaged in small-scale looting; he didn't care to enquire.

He made a cursory search of the drawers and cupboards, finding only the predictable possessions of a single man living abroad: clothes, cameras, a selection of records and tapes, some paperback books. A sideboard drawer held a small pile of correspondence, official-looking and in Spanish. Rebecca identified it as bank statements, bills, letters from lawyers and accountants and, at the bottom, letters referring to the purchase of the villa.

There was no personal correspondence at all. Either Norris had destroyed it or the police had taken it.

Harry came to the bedroom, thought of the album of press-cuttings and went to the bedside cabinet. Which was now empty.

'Alan has it,' said Rebecca, who had followed him into the bedroom and seen what he was after.

'Alan Mullins?'

'Yes. He took it away with him after the body was found. He said he thought there was no point in stirring things up more than they were already.' Seeing the doubt in Harry's eyes, she added, 'I think he's right. And I'm sure we can get it back from him if you want it. In fact, he's already asked me if I want it, but of course I don't. It's the last bloody thing I want, is that.'

Harry nodded. Anyway, he'd seen the album and knew what it contained. In Alan Mullins's shoes, he might have done the same and spirited it out of harm's way.

Rebecca reclined on the bed while he completed his search, discovering only piles of handkerchiefs and underwear, a wardrobe full of shirts and slacks and odd items of jewellery.

'So,' she said, watching him close the last of the drawers, 'what are our deductions?'

'He got pissed and fell in the swimming-pool.'

'I don't believe that.'

'I know you don't.'

'And neither do you.'

He shrugged, not sure what he believed. Nor caring much while there were other, more urgent matters to claim his attention. He sat on the bed and took her hand.

'You remember the last time we were in here?'

'And I had to remind you of all those people outside the door . . . ?'

He nodded. 'They're not there now.'

She looked at him. 'If you mean you want to screw me and would I mind, then the answer's no, I wouldn't.'

As they slipped out of their clothes and came together under the thin, cotton sheet, he wondered which of them was using the other. Was she offering herself to him as reward for his feeble attempts at investigation? And had he been going through the motions simply in order to get her to the bed they were at last sharing? Perhaps, duplicitous bastards both, they deserved one another.

9.

Gerald Fieldhouse turned up on the beach the next morning and strolled disconsolately over to where Jill was preoccupied with her book and Harry with thoughts of Rebecca and their love-making. It puzzled him that he felt no guilt, only concern that Jill shouldn't be upset by ever finding out what had happened. It didn't seem to him that he loved her any the less for having loved the other woman.

Fieldhouse was wearing jeans, a short-sleeved shirt and plastic sandals and looked over-dressed among the well-oiled flesh around him.

'Hi,' Harry greeted him. 'How're you?'

'All right,' he said, though he didn't look it. His face was tired, his eyes swollen beneath the sun-tan. 'Rebecca said you wanted to talk to me.'

'How's Samantha?' said Jill, looking up at him.

He shrugged. 'Not a lot different.'

'Do you fancy a drink?' said Harry, getting to his feet and nodding towards the ramshackle restaurant where they might be able to have a quiet word away from the sun-worshippers and, more particularly, away from Jill.

'If you like.' His tone suggested they might as well waste their time there as waste it anywhere else.

'Do you want anything bringing back?' Harry asked Jill.

'No, thanks,' she said, rewarding his attentiveness with a grateful smile. She flashed a glance at Fieldhouse as if to say – observe how a couple should behave.

Harry and Fieldhouse crossed the beach to the bar, Fieldhouse eyeing the bikinis and Harry trying to think what he might ask him that he didn't know already. He ordered two beers and decided that Fieldhouse, a declared *aficionado* of the Spanish national sport, might appreciate it if he took the bull by the horns.

'Do you think Norris's death was accidental?'

It took him by surprise. 'Do I what?'

'Do you think Norris's death was accidental?'

'Sure, yes,' he said, guarded. 'What else?'

Harry spelled it out. 'Well, if it wasn't accidental, it means somebody killed him.'

'Like who?'

'I've no idea,' said Harry, wondering how he'd come to be answering the questions instead of asking them. 'Do you know if he'd got himself involved in anything over here?'

'Like what?'

'Like drugs. Anything. Anything that might have got him into bother.'

Fieldhouse shook his head. 'Not that I know of.'

'He hadn't got on the wrong side of anybody? Any of the locals for instance?'

Again: 'Not that I know of.'

'So you'd go along with it being an accident. No question.'

'Sure.' Then, finally, he began to talk: 'I'll tell you something, though. That bird of his is off her rocker. I mean I saw him, right? I was there. I helped pull him out of the fucking pool. Whereas she wasn't there. She was miles away. So how come she thinks she knows better than anybody else what happened?'

'I don't think she's claiming that,' said Harry patiently.

'Oh no? So why all this? Why all the fucking questions?'

'She just thinks there are one or two strange things about the way he died.'

'Like what?'

Challenged, Harry found himself floundering. 'Well, like . . . why did he want to have a party anyway?'

'I don't know. Same reason anybody ever wants to have a party I suppose.'

'And why was he putting the booze away like he was?'

''Cause he was thirsty. 'Cause he had to stand around talking to all them fucking wankers and it made him thirsty.'

'Yes, OK,' said Harry, who was beginning to feel he'd be better off banging his head against a brick wall. 'So you think it was an accident.'

'Yes. And not just me neither. The cops here, they think the same, don't they?'

'Looks like it,' Harry admitted.

'Well, then.'

Harry gave up and concentrated on finishing his drink. Then he found that Fieldhouse still had a grievance to express.

'I just hope she's not putting it about that I had anything to do with it.'

'Rebecca . . . ?'

'Yes. 'Cause I wouldn't take kindly to that. I wouldn't take kindly to that at all.'

The threat was clear enough. To Rebecca and, by association, to himself. He straightened up from the bar and turned till he was facing the other man.

'There's nobody putting that about,' he said evenly.

'So why all these questions? What's all this third-degree stuff about?'

'I've told you. Rebecca wanted to be sure it was an accident.'

''Course it was a fucking accident!'

'So you said.'

'Well, then,' said Fieldhouse, running out of steam.

Harry drained his glass. 'See you around.'

'Sure. Must get together some time.' Neither meant it. Each would avoid the other like the plague. Harry put down his glass and turned away. But Fieldhouse was muttering, just loud enough to claim his attention: 'And you know what they say about people who live in glass houses . . . '

Harry stopped and stared. Fieldhouse gave a sickly sort of grin and repeated, 'You know what they say about—'

'I do, yes. What about it?'

'Well, if it wasn't an accident . . . I mean just say for the sake of argument that it wasn't a fucking accident . . . '

'Yes?'

'I'll tell you who might have had a motive, shall I?' Harry

106

suddenly guessed what was coming, but was powerless to do other than stand and hear him out. 'I mean from what I saw . . . and Sam'll bear me out on this . . . things weren't all that sweet between Norris and his bird. Not all that sweet at all.'

'So?'

Fieldhouse held up his hands in a gesture of helplessness. '*I'm* not saying anything. 'Cause I think it was an accident, right?'

'You said.'

'But if I didn't. And if I was wanting to point the finger . . . which, like I say, I'm not . . . '

'For Christ's sake . . . ' muttered Harry, who wanted more than anything to punch him in the mouth.

'Then I'd say she had as good a motive as anybody,' said Fieldhouse, taking a quick step backwards, out of the danger area. 'I'd say it's Rebecca you want to be talking to. On account of maybe she ended up hating Norris so much that she paid somebody to do the job.'

An interview with the doctor who had attended Norris and declared him dead was more difficult to arrange but could hardly be less fruitful. Identifying him was straight-forward enough. There were few doctors in the area who were available for emergency calls, fewer still who also specialised in treating foreign visitors. The second one Rebecca contacted was the right one. He admitted readily enough to having been called out on the night of Norris's death and, indeed, to having the body still in his mortuary.

However he was a busy man and, unlike Alan Mullins and Gerald Fieldhouse, wasn't going to trot down to the beach to chat to Harry at his convenience. Instead, Harry would have to attend at the doctor's convenience, waiting around until he had time to spare between treating tourists suffering from diarrhoea or gastro-enteritis.

In the meantime Harry and Jill visited the city of Malaga, climbing to the ruined Moorish fortress and then coming down again to tramp around the cathedral and the market. Harry enjoyed the strangeness of it all, while Jill, taking photographs and eager for information, seemed envious of the locals for being local and not tourists as they were.

He also managed a meeting with Rebecca at the Café Ricco, where she explained to him about the doctor.

'And did you see Gerald? I told him to find you.'

Harry nodded. 'For what good it did me.'

She understood. 'In one of his moods, was he?'

'When is he ever in anything else?'

'And how's Jill?'

'Oh . . . fine. Enjoying the holiday.'

She looked at him and laughed. 'You must feel like the cat that's getting the cream. With both of us at your beck and call.'

'I don't,' he said shortly.

'Oh, sorry,' she said in mock-apology. 'You mean you're not enjoying yourself?'

He wondered whether he was. In truth, he felt like a tight-rope walker, inching along unsteadily, wondering when the fall would come and on which side to land when it did.

The doctor who had attended Norris was Doctor Natras, who ran the Clinic Of All The Saints on the outskirts of Marbella. Following Rebecca's instructions, Harry found himself in a waiting-room lined by elegant prints and full of brown leather sofas. A cheery Scottish nurse took his name and then ignored him for an hour and a half, ushering a stream of English and German patients ahead of him. He had begun to doze when she finally announced: 'The Doctor will see you now, Mr Sommers.'

'Thanks,' said Harry, standing.

'Sorry you've had to wait. We've had rather a busy morning.'

She led him into a room that was more office than surgery, save for a wash-basin in one corner and a screen blocking off another. Doctor Natras was in his late thirties, an Anglo-Indian. He was dressed in a grey suit and white shirt with a tie that had a yacht motif inscribed above a set of initials. He rose to meet Harry, shook his hand and repeated the nurse's apology for the time he'd had to wait.

'That's all right,' said Harry, whose job had accustomed him to waiting. 'It's good of you to see me.'

Doctor Natras smiled and nodded in agreement. He spread his hands on the top of his desk. 'And so how can I help you?'

'It's about Norris Edgerton.'

'Yes.'

'I'm making a few enquiries on behalf of some friends of his.'

'Friends . . . ?'

'Yes,' said Harry stubbornly.

Doctor Natras hesitated, then smiled and fluttered a hand. 'Go ahead.'

'What time did you receive the call asking you to go to the villa?'

'At ten minutes to three in the morning.'

'Can you remember who made the call?'

'Not the name, no. But it was one of the two men who were waiting there when I arrived.'

'What did they say had happened? I mean, what were their exact words as far as you can remember them?'

The Doctor's expression said that he couldn't guarantee exact words but would do his best. 'They said there had been an accident and that someone had drowned. I asked them where they were calling from, and they gave me the address.'

'And when you got there . . . ?'

'When I got there I found, in short, that they were right.'

'He'd drowned? It was as simple as that?'

'I'm not sure why you regard drowning as simple.'

'There was no other possible cause of death?'

'No. In my opinion, it was a case of primary drowning.' He smiled and explained: 'Primary drowning is where the victim is already dead when he is pulled from the water. Secondary drowning is where he is still alive but dies subsequently from the effects of the water. This was a case of primary drowning.'

'And you've no doubt about that?'

'None. Why? Do you have reason to doubt?'

'Not really. I just want to be sure, that's all.' Though still on Rebecca's side, he was finding it increasingly difficult to share her conviction that there'd been foul play. 'And the post-mortem confirmed this, did it?'

Doctor Natras went through a small pantomime of surprise. 'Post-mortem? There was no post-mortem.'

'No?'

'The investigating judge didn't ask for one. He saw no reason to ask for one.'

'I see.'

'All that was requested was that I take a sample of blood. Which I did. This was then analysed – not by me but by the police laboratories . . . '

'Yes.'

'And was found to contain a blood alcohol level of over three hundred per cent.'

'That's high . . . ?'

'Very high.'

It sounds it, thought Harry. It also sounded more and more like the open-and-shut case the Spanish police claimed it to be. He wondered how far he'd been mesmerised by Rebecca into seeing suspicious circumstances which, without her influence, he would have immediately dismissed as mere coincidence and the product of an over-active imagination.

'Well, thank you, Doctor,' he said. 'I think you've answered all my questions.'

'You're not the only one who's been asking them.'

'No?' said Harry, intrigued.

Doctor Natras smiled, enjoying his little surprise. 'Oh no. I had visitors yesterday and I have a visitor today. All wanting to know the same things as yourself.'

'Who?'

'I don't know whether I should tell you.'

'Well, of course, I'd treat it as confidential,' urged Harry, becoming irritated by Natras's tantalising manner.

'All right. I suppose it can do no harm. I was visited yesterday by two detectives from your Scotland Yard.'

Of course. He should have expected that. 'And what did they want?'

'The same as everybody else. To know how he died. And then there were certain formalities of identification, a copy of the death certificate . . . things of that sort for them to take back.'

'And were they . . . satisfied?'

'They seemed to me extremely satisfied.'

'Who were the other visitors?'

'Just one,' Natras corrected him. 'Just one more. And she's still here at the moment in fact.' Harry waited patiently. 'Mrs Edgerton. The wife of the deceased.'

This time he couldn't have expected it. He knew from Rebecca that Norris had a wife but had dismissed her as part of his old life, left behind in England. It hadn't occurred to him she might wish to assert her rightful place beside his coffin.

'She's come over from England?'

'She flew over this morning, and now has come here to view the body. I would suppose that her motives are more emotional than those of the Scotland Yard detectives. Would you like me to ask her if she will see you?'

'Yes,' he said on impulse. 'If you wouldn't mind.'

He didn't relish confronting Norris's widow, but experience had taught him how information could come from the most unlikely sources. Having come this far, he might as well see the job through.

'I'll say you were a friend of her husband's, shall I?'

Harry nodded. The Scottish nurse was sent for and was instructed by Doctor Natras to ask Mrs Edgerton if she wouldn't mind speaking to a friend of her husband. It appeared she didn't mind at all, and Harry, after thanking Doctor Natras for his time and shaking hands again, was shown into another, smaller room where a short, stout woman was sipping at a cup of coffee and smoking a cigarette. She was wearing a blue suit, and a black chiffon scarf as a sign of her mourning.

The nurse introduced them and left, closing the door behind her.

'I'm sorry about what happened,' Harry began cautiously, wondering whether she was liable to burst into tears. 'It must have been a terrible shock.'

'Not really.'

'No . . . ?'

'After the way he'd lived, I could hardly be surprised at the way he died.'

'Well . . . '

'And, as for shocks, I should be used to them by now. I've been married to him for twenty years and I don't think there's been one of 'em that hasn't had its share of shocks in it.'

Evidently she wasn't going to burst into tears. Her manner was hostile, though Harry didn't feel it to be personally so. It was more as if she mistrusted everyone on policy.

'And you were a friend of his, were you?'

He decided she might appreciate an honest answer. 'I'm just over here on holiday and got to know him.'

'So why do you want to talk to me?'

'Some friends of his were . . . well, just wanting to be sure that what happened really was an accident.'

She stared at him. 'Are you police?'

'No. I work as a private detective in London. Only, like I say, I'm over here on holiday. There's nothing . . . nothing official about this.'

'You think somebody killed him?'

'I wouldn't put it like that. It's more a matter of making sure that nobody did.'

She took time to think about it, lighting another cigarette from the stub of her old one.

'Would you rather I went?' offered Harry.

'What the hell does it matter anyway? No, you ask me what you like. Though I know bugger-all, I'll tell you that from the start.'

The small room was full of her cigarette smoke and unpleasantly warm. He felt sorry for her, seeing how difficult this must be, coming to mourn her husband in the country of his exile. He determined to be brief and to the point.

'While Norris was over here, did you keep in touch?'

'Depends what you mean by in touch. He sent the odd post-card, Christmas card, not much else.'

'So you wouldn't know much about the people he knew over here?'

'No.'

'Did he send you money?'

She hesitated, then admitted, 'Now and again. What's this got to do with what happened to him?'

'I just want a general picture,' said Harry apologetically.

'Then you'd be better off talking to somebody else.'

'Did he have any enemies?'

'Hundreds.'

'I mean anybody that might have . . . might have wanted to harm him?'

'Wanted to kill him you mean. Oh, I don't know. And, quite frankly, I don't want to know.'

Perhaps she was more distressed than he'd given her credit for, or even yet been able to admit to herself. Certainly she was becoming agitated under his questioning.

'I can understand how you must feel . . . ' he said.

'I doubt it.'

So she didn't want sympathy. He might as well plough on.

'Has anybody ever approached you, asking about him?'

'It depends when you mean. Once upon a time they never stopped.'

'Recently.'

'Not recently, no. Why should they? Everybody knows where he is.' Then, realising what she'd said: 'And they certainly know now if they didn't know before.'

Harry could only nod. She seemed to be calming down again.

'You come from London, do you?' she asked.

'Me? Yes.'

'I thought so. Could tell by the accent. Norris came from Clapham. You know Clapham?'

'Sort of.'

'We lived there for five years when we were first married.'

'Where do you live now?' asked Harry, deciding to settle for small talk since his questions had got him nowhere.

'A place called Palmer's Heath, just outside Windsor. You

113

won't know it, I don't suppose . . . ?' Harry shook his head. 'It's very nice. Very quiet. Somewhere Norris always thought he could retire to when . . . well, when he'd got enough money, that was the plan. Always full of plans, he was.' She seemed to be talking as much for her own benefit as his, composing herself. She tapped the ash from her cigarette, uncrossed her legs and tugged her skirt down to her knees. 'Can I ask you something, Mr . . . ?'

'Sommers. Harry Sommers. Yes, sure.'

'Did he have, you know . . . other women?'

'Other women . . . ?' stalled Harry, thinking immediately of Rebecca and feeling his own position, already questionable, become distinctly squalid.

'Oh, I'm sure he must have had. I mean he was over here long enough. I didn't expect him to live like a monk. But was there anybody special? Anybody he'd become fond of?'

'Like I say, I didn't know him very long . . . '

But she wasn't so easily evaded. 'No, well, you wouldn't have had to know him long. I would have thought it'd be fairly obvious whether he was accompanied or not.'

Her eyes were now sharp and on him. Despite her black chiffon of mourning, she was clearly determined on remembering Norris with all his worldly imperfections and was relying on Harry to fill in the details.

'He didn't have a regular girl-friend, no. At least not one I was aware of.'

She didn't believe him. 'He must have changed, then.'

'Perhaps he had. I didn't know him for very long. And now I really have got to go. Are you all right? Is there anything I can do to help while you're over here?'

She shook her head. 'I'm being well taken care of, thank you. There's this lawyer Norris had – he's arranging everything for me.'

'Good. Well, like I say, I'm sorry about everything that's happened.'

But Mrs Edgerton's thoughts were elsewhere. 'I believe there were two detectives from Scotland Yard came to have a look at him.'

114

'So I've been told.'

'Never forget, do they? You'd think they'd lose interest, but they never do. Like elephants.'

'Did you meet them?'

'No.' She came near to shuddering at the thought. 'It wasn't me they wanted to see. Just him. Wouldn't be satisfied until they'd seen him laid out.' Then she gave an unexpected smile. 'Still, they never got him, did they? Never managed to lock him away, which is what they'd most like to have done.'

It was a thought that seemed to give her some consolation. Harry left her with it, glad to escape and feeling that his task was now over. He had conducted an investigation of a sort which had allied him with Rebecca and made them lovers. Otherwise it had left him no wiser than when he'd started, save for a growing feeling that the truth had probably passed beyond everyone's reach and would accompany Norris into his grave.

The funeral was the following afternoon at the small Anglican church of Saint John the Baptist in the western sector of Marbella. There was to be a short service, with nothing said about the life and achievements of the deceased, before burial in the cemetery beside the church.

It was about the same time that Harry drove Jill into Marbella for her hair appointment with Mats, the Swedish hairdresser. He then walked along the promenade in search of the Café Fortuna, which turned out to be an unpretentious bar dominated by a hissing coffee-machine and a television screen which showed people talking round a table but had the sound turned down. As arranged, Rebecca was already there, reading a Spanish newspaper.

'Hi,' he said.

She lowered her paper and raised her face for a kiss.

'Do you want another coffee?' he asked since her cup was almost empty.

'Cappuchino.'

He ordered two cappuchinos at the counter. 'He'll bring them over,' Rebecca called, and so he returned and sat down at

115

the table with her. She completed folding up her newspaper, dropped it into a bag beside her chair and then smiled across at him.

'And how're you?'

'Fine. How're you?'

'OK. Norris should be buried by now.'

Harry glanced instinctively at his watch and saw it was two-thirty, which he knew anyway since that was the time they had planned to meet when he'd phoned to tell her of Jill's convenient hair-appointment.

'You're not going, then,' he said.

'Of course I'm not bloody going. For one thing I'm not all that keen on funerals generally, and for another his sodding wife's going to be there.'

Harry nodded. 'I met her.'

'You did? When? And what's she like?'

He gave her an account of his meeting at the doctor's, though found it harder to explain the impression Mrs Edgerton had made on him. 'She seemed fairly ordinary. Wanted to know things about Norris. I think she was probably more upset than she was letting on.' No point in mentioning how she'd quizzed him about the ladies in Norris's life.

'What did the doctor have to say?'

'He agreed with the police. No sign of foul play. Everything was as Alan and Gerald had told it. Norris was already dead when he got there, and they were the only two present.'

Rebecca pulled a little face. 'Very cosy. In other words, he doesn't want to rock the boat either.'

'There hasn't been a post-mortem,' continued Harry, 'because the police haven't asked for one. But he has taken a sample of blood that showed Norris to be well over the limit.'

'So what do we do now?'

'Nothing,' he said firmly.

'What?' she exclaimed in dismay. 'You mean give up?'

'There's nothing more we can do. There's no evidence. There's not going to be any. They're burying him, and that's an end of it.'

116

The more he'd thought about the case, the more he could no longer ignore the obvious: that Norris had got pissed and then drowned in his own swimming-pool. As simple as that. Rebecca's scepticism was largely based on Norris's peculiar behaviour towards her, and that had been plausibly explained by Alan Mullins as nothing more sinister than an affair coming to its close. Fieldhouse, taking things further, had suggested that Rebecca had as good a motive for wanting to bump him off as any of them. Well, no, he wasn't going seriously to consider that, but it did serve as a reminder that Rebecca was far from impartial. Everybody else thought Norris had died by accident, and he was inclined to agree with them.

'I see,' she said, not liking it.

'Accept it,' he urged quietly.

But she was defiant. 'No. I didn't believe it when it happened and I don't believe it now.'

'Because you don't want to.'

She reacted sharply. 'And what the hell do you mean by that?'

'You want it to be a murder. It's more exciting that way. More glamorous than having to face that he got tanked up on vodka and fell in.'

'Well, thank you,' she said quietly. For a moment he thought she was about to walk out on him.

'I was the same,' he said, trying to soothe her. 'I went along with you to start with.'

'Only now you want to chicken out.'

He ignored that. 'I was suspicious to start with. So, because you asked me to, I went and talked to people. I've talked to Mullins, talked to Fieldhouse, and to you. Then yesterday I talked to that doctor and even to Norris's wife, for Christ's sake. And there's been nothing come out of it to support those suspicions. Everybody agrees he died by accident. All the evidence—'

'What evidence?' she interrupted.

'Well, no, there isn't much,' he admitted. 'But he was drunk. Very drunk. His blood sample confirms that. And there's no evidence to the contrary. That's what I'm saying. You can't keep on being suspicious when everything points the other way. Well, maybe you can, but I can't.'

Besides, he'd so far been lucky; the Spanish authorities didn't seem to have got wind of what he'd been up to. Should he push that luck and carry on, he might well end up once again behind the thick walls of the police-station, only this time facing a different sort of reception.

'So you're telling me I'm stupid,' she said.

'No.'

'Well, that's what it amounts to.'

'I'm telling you we were both wrong.'

'So we're both stupid.'

'If you like.'

'Well, I don't agree,' she said calmly. 'But if you want to give up, then you give up.'

'That doesn't mean I want to give up on you.'

'No?'

'No way.'

'You're a brave man. I mean considering what happened to my last lover, don't you think I might be some kind of jinx?'

But she was now flirting again. He realised with relief he'd been forgiven for abandoning the case. To confirm this, they finished their cappuchinos, then went back to her flat, which was a one-room apartment in a tower-block, almost as small as she'd described it. They went to bed and spent the afternoon there till it was time for him to go and meet Jill.

Suddenly the holiday was shrinking fast, with no more than a few days to go. They continued to visit the beach, though for shorter sessions now time no longer seemed infinite and there were still Ronda and Mijas to be visited.

Jill seemed contented and relaxed, though she was reading even more than usual, so that he wondered if she were using the books as a barrier between them. Once she'd exhausted the supply brought with her, she turned to whatever she could find in the racks of the local *supermercado*: thrillers and five-hundred-page sagas of Californian family life that she would have dismissed disdainfully at home. They avoided the Café Ricco and hardly mentioned all that had occurred in those first turbulent days of their vacation.

He snatched just one more meeting with Rebecca, when Jill wanted to spend time shopping in Marbella. A furtive phone-call to the Hertz Rent-A-Car office, and Rebecca was again waiting for him at the Café Fortuna. They talked about how long she would stay in her present job or even stay in Spain at all.

'I don't suppose you're likely to turn up in London . . . ?' asked Harry.

'I don't suppose I am. Why? What would you do if I did?' Then, as he wondered the same, she added: 'Anyway, no, so let's not waste time talking about it.'

He took one of the Agency cards from his wallet. 'You can always give me a ring if you feel like it.'

She shrugged, read what was on the card and dropped it into her bag. 'I'd better warn you, I'm not very good at staying in touch and all that crap. So best forget about it, Harry. Let's just say it was good while it lasted. Have a good life, OK?'

She leant over and kissed him. He saw to his surprise she was about to leave.

'Won't I see you again?'

'No. I'm working for the rest of the week, and you . . . well, you've got other commitments.'

He knew he must let her go and that she was wise in the way she was playing it, keeping things light and aiming for a quick exit. But still, there were things he wanted to say.

'Look after yourself and . . . well, I hope you find that millionaire,' was how it came out. What he really wanted to say was that she should rate herself more highly and make others do the same. But she was already at the door of the café, giving him a final wave. '*Ciao.*' And then she was gone.

Their plane was due to leave at 3.30 in the afternoon. To allow time for returning the hire-car and checking in, they planned to leave by midday. Once breakfast was over, they began packing and tidying up the villa. Jill was already becoming nervous and preoccupied at the prospect of the flight. Harry went outside to stack away the sunbeds and garden furniture, so she was closer to the phone and answered it when it rang.

He heard her exchanging pleasantries and wondered who it could be. Then he heard, 'Would you like to speak to Harry?' and a moment later she appeared on the patio. 'Phone for you.'

'Who is it?'

'Rebecca.'

He gave a grunt of surprise, genuine enough, which he hoped hid the excitement that had come with the mention of her name. He picked up the receiver, noting that Jill had left the room.

'Hello?'

'You don't have to sound so defensive. I told her I just wanted to say goodbye to the pair of you, which she seemed to think was quite a charming idea.'

'So do I.'

'Yes, well, something else as well. I've got a new lead on Norris's death.'

He held his breath. 'What?'

'Well, I haven't got it all sorted yet. But the point is he'd been doing some very strange things with his money before he died. Drawing out big amounts for no obvious reason.'

Harry relaxed. It already sounded less like the 'new lead' that she'd promised than another case of her imagination working overtime.

'Is that all?'

'What do you mean, is that all?' she retorted, annoyed. 'It's more than you ever bloody managed!'

'All right, but how do you know about Norris's financial affairs anyway?'

'Ah well, I've met this extraordinarily talented young man. Who just happens to be a tax lawyer. And who I've managed to persuade to do one or two favours for me.'

He could imagine well enough the manner of her persuasion.

Just as she'd teased Harry into working for her, so she'd now got some other poor fool drooling over her and willing to do anything in the hope it might end with him bedding her.

'Tell him he has my sympathy.'

'Oh, fuck off, then,' she said, and put down the phone.

He thought about ringing her back, decided against it, put down his own receiver and went to join Jill in the bedroom where she had the half-filled suitcases spread open before her on the bed.

'Nice of her to ring,' she said brightly. 'She sounds as though she's got over the dreadful way that her boy-friend died.'

'Well, I don't think he was all that special. Just one in a very long line, I shouldn't be surprised.' She shot him a quick glance, but he concentrated on the line of his shirts hanging in the wardrobe. 'Are any of these hangers ours?'

10.

Spring had come to London during their absence. The downpours had dwindled to occasional showers. The tops of the trees, swaying in the blustery wind, were flecked with buds.

Jill returned to school for the start of what she called the summer term. Harry resumed his life of process-serving and surveillance. He was secretly pleased to be back in harness, though to anyone who asked he insisted he'd had a marvellous time and would give anything to be there still. The sudden death of Norris and his own brief fling with Rebecca had seemed to slide away into the irretrievable past the moment they fastened their seat-belts ready for take-off.

Though what did remain, besides the yet-to-be-developed photographs and the glowing tans, was a noticeable reserve on Jill's part whenever that aspect of the holiday was mentioned. As though there were questions she longed to ask and yet dared not.

Yvonne, with no such inhibitions, wanted to know everything.

'Well, you've seen the sun and no mistake,' she greeted Harry on his first day back. 'Now tell me all about it. What was the villa like? Did it live up to expectations?'

He gave her a blow-by-blow account, including the criminal histories of their holiday companions and the snatching of Jill's handbag. 'How dreadful . . . !' she exclaimed, aghast. By the time he had recounted Norris's death and his own gentle inquisition at the police-station, she was listening in stunned silence. He laughed at her amazed expression, then remembered the present he'd bought her and had to run out again, down the stairs and past the dry-cleaner's to where his car was parked. Acting on Jill's advice, he had bought her a bracelet, with which she was delighted, fastening it on her pudgy wrist.

'But tell me about this poor man who fell in his own

swimming-pool,' she urged. 'Did the police really do nothing?'

'Next to nothing. I think they were just happy he was off their patch.'

'Oh, but that's terrible.'

'Well, I think they were probably right, as it happens. It was an accident, and there wasn't much anybody could do about it.' It now all seemed a great distance away, a small incident on foreign soil. Difficult to remember why he'd once been so concerned about it. 'And what about you?' he asked. 'How's business?'

She brought him up-to-date on the small triumphs and set-backs that had occurred during his absence: Samuels, Jessop and King, the neighbouring solicitors, had more leg-work awaiting him; there'd been an enquiry by a local bookie who suspected his staff of dipping into the till; and one of the divorce cases on their books had been brought to an unprofitable close with the reconciliation of the warring couple. They got out his diary and decided how he should best divide his time.

'I bet you wish you'd never come back,' joked Yvonne as the blank space began to fill.

'You're not kidding. For two pins I'd be back on that plane tomorrow.'

In truth, though, he felt himself to be where he belonged, among the jumbled streets of London where sunshine and parking-spaces were at a premium. This was real and solid, besides which the white villas of the Costa del Sol were a side-show and not the genuine article. He thought only occasionally of Rebecca Connors mooching around the marina at Porto Banus in her Hertz Rent-A-Car tee-shirt.

It was a few days before he found it convenient to drop in at the New Oasis Club and return the keys of the villa to Leo Shapiro. Although late morning, the porno cinema was already open for business.

'You looking for Mr Shapiro?' asked the woman in the horn-rimmed glasses, recognising Harry.

'If he's about.'

'He's in the club. Go on through.'

Harry did and found Leo Shapiro at a table, counting the previous night's takings. There was no sign of Dave the barman, but from outside came the sound of crates being piled one upon another.

Shapiro greeted Harry like a long-lost brother, insisting he had a drink, though Harry, with a crowded day, was in a hurry to be off. Still, he owed the man something – the keys he'd just placed on the table were evidence of that – so he accepted the drink, sat down and told Shapiro that, yes, the villa had been wonderful, luxurious, out of this world.

Shapiro laughed gleefully. 'What did I tell you? And you didn't believe me, did you? Now be honest, Harry boy. You thought it was going to be some flea-ridden shack!'

'It was nice. Very nice. I only wish I could afford one.'

'Who says I can afford it? I own it, OK. Doesn't mean I can afford it.' They both laughed at the joke, then he became serious. 'And what about Norris? You met Norris, didn't you? Wasn't that terrible?'

'Diabolical,' agreed Harry, wondering how Shapiro came to be so well up on events in southern Spain.

'And you were at the party?'

'Yes.'

'He was drinking a lot, was he?'

'A fair amount. But he was still on his feet. I mean he didn't seem too bad when I last saw him.'

'Terrible. I've been talking to his wife. She told me how she bumped into you over there.'

So there was his answer. Shapiro had spoken to Mrs Edgerton. As simple as that. Why was it everything surrounding Norris's death first struck him as suspicious and then revealed itself to be perfectly straightforward?

'Yes, I saw her when she was over there for the funeral. In fact, she'd just been to see his body so she wasn't looking too happy.'

'She's a tough cookie is Lesley. She'll get over it.'

'I'm sure she will,' agreed Harry, remembering how his

sympathetic approach had been put down.

'I gather you were asking questions, conducting some kind of investigation . . . ?'

'Kind of,' said Harry, thinking well, of course, she would have told him that as well.

'Why? Just keeping your hand in or what?'

'Some people didn't think the police were doing enough,' said Harry with a dismissive shrug. 'So they asked me – God knows why . . . '

'Because you're a private dick,' said Shapiro.

'Well, yes. So they asked me if I'd just check and make sure there hadn't been anything underhand, anything the police were covering up.'

'And was there?' He seemed amused by the notion.

'No,' said Harry shortly.

'I hope it didn't spoil the holiday.'

'It didn't.'

'It was that bird of his who was curious, was it?' He saw Harry's hesitation and smiled, pleased with his surprise. 'That blonde piece he was knocking off? She was the one getting her knickers in a twist?'

He hadn't got that from Mrs Edgerton. Not unless she'd known a good deal more than she was letting on when Harry had spoken to her.

'See, I know these things, Harry,' said Shapiro, smiling. 'I like to keep in touch. That way I don't get any nasty surprises.'

Harry said nothing and finished his drink. He left the club without learning who Shapiro had spoken to but not caring much either. It had probably been Mullins or Fieldhouse. Yet again there was no great mystery.

Forget it, he told himself, coming outside into the fresh air. Forget Norris, forget Rebecca, forget the whole show. It seemed like a simple prescription for happiness, and he resolved to follow it.

It was evening by the time he got back to the office. To his surprise, Yvonne was still there, drinking tea and reading a

125

copy of *Cosmopolitan*.

'I thought you'd have been off home.'

'I would have been,' she said, 'but I wanted to catch you. There's been a friend of yours called.'

'Friend . . . ?'

'A young lady.' She consulted her note-pad. 'Rebecca Connors.'

Harry stared. 'Called . . . ? You mean she rang?'

'No. She came here. Came to the office. Some time about . . . oh, about one o'clock it must have been.'

His heart raced at the news, betraying all his resolutions about forgetting her. Then came the rush of questions: what had she been doing here? Why should she be seeking him out after her stark declaration that their affair was over and done with? And did any of it matter so long as it meant he'd be seeing her again?

'You do know who she is?' said Yvonne, watching him.

'Oh . . . yes. Sure.'

'She said you met her in Spain.'

'I did.' Then corrected that to: 'We did.'

'She didn't look as though she came from round here, I must say.' She unwrapped a toffee and slipped it into her mouth.

'What did she want?' he asked, trying to sound casual.

'Well, she wanted to see you. Then when I said you weren't here, she wanted to know where you were, but, of course, I couldn't say for certain.'

'Did she leave a message or . . . ? I mean what did she say?'

'Well, at first she said she'd wait. But I could see she wasn't going to wait long, she was that fidgety. Couldn't sit still for two minutes together.' She paused to chew at her toffee.

'So she went?' he prompted, impatient to know how he might find her.

'Yes. Said she couldn't wait any longer. Which, like I say, hadn't really been very long . . . '

'Did she leave a message?' Harry interrupted.

'I was just going to tell you that.'

It was a mild rebuke for his impatience. She tore off the top sheet of her pad and handed it to him.

'REBECCA CONNORS,' he read. 'MAJORS HOTEL. KNIGHTSBRIDGE. 334-8764.'

'That's where she's staying. She said she was going back there and would stay there till she heard from you.'

'Right. Thanks,' said Harry, heading for the privacy of his own office. 'I'll give her a ring.'

'She said something else as well.'

'What?'

Yvonne gave a mischievous smile. 'She said to tell you she's a better detective than you are.'

'I shouldn't be surprised.'

'She says that she's solved the mystery.'

There was only one mystery he could think of. 'About Norris's death?' he asked, intrigued.

'Whose?'

'What I was telling you about this morning. The bloke I met over there who had a record as long as your arm . . . '

'Oh, him.'

'And then managed to drown himself.'

'I don't know. That was all she said. That she was a better detective than you are and that she'd solved the mystery.'

Harry nodded and went through the door into his own poky little office. She's solved the mystery, he thought, as he dialled out the number from the piece of paper. With the help of her tax lawyer friend no doubt. Had they discovered foul play after all? The phone began to ring at the other end. And why did she have to travel so far to bring him news of it?

'Majors Hotel. Good evening.'

'I want to speak to one of your guests.'

'Yes, sir.'

'It's a Miss Rebecca Connors. I don't know her room number.'

There was a pause. When the girl spoke again, her cool, automatic manner had gone; in its place was alarm or fright, Harry wasn't sure which. 'Rebecca Connors?'

'Yes.'

Another pause. 'Hello?' said Harry, wondering if they'd been cut off.

Then he heard a man's voice: 'Who's that speaking please?'

Now it was his turn to feel alarmed, though he still hoped it might be a crossed line or some other easily explained cause for the confusion.

'I want to speak to Rebecca Connors,' he repeated.

'Yes. And who're you?'

It wasn't a crossed line. It was something else, though what he didn't yet dare to guess. 'Never mind who I am. Is Rebecca Connors staying there or not?'

'I'm sorry, sir.' The voice was firm and authoritative. 'I can't tell you anything until you identify yourself.'

Harry hesitated but knew he had no option. 'My name's Harry Sommers. I'm a friend of Miss Connors. Now what the hell's going on?'

It was a three-quarters-of-an-hour drive across the city. He did it in twenty-eight minutes, parking on the double yellow lines outside the hotel, behind the jumble of police cars and motorcycles. The ambulance had already gone.

Inside, the small foyer was crowded. Harry looked around wildly and received curious glances in reply from some of those who were waiting. There was a policeman standing by the lifts.

'Detective Inspector Porterhouse . . . ?' Harry blurted at him.

'What about him?' said the policeman, who had boyish features and an off-hand manner.

'Where do I find him?' His desperation gave the question the force of a threat.

The policeman flinched slightly. 'You could try over there,' he said, nodding towards the reception desk.

Harry pushed his way through to it and repeated his demand. A flustered receptionist took his name and asked him to wait. As he did so, he thought of how Rebecca must have come to that desk to collect her key only hours earlier after returning from his office where she'd failed to find him. He gave an audible moan of despair, then someone was saying his name and raising the flap so he could pass through. He was directed to a half-open door which had 'Manager' on it. He pushed it and walked in. A tall, balding man was standing by the desk and speaking into the telephone. He looked up when Harry entered, said, 'Sit down', and continued his phone conversation.

'You're Harry Sommers,' he said, when he'd finished.

'Yes.'

'I'm the one you spoke to on the phone. Detective Inspector Porterhouse. Thanks for coming.'

'Is she . . . ?'

He knew already, had had it spelled out to him by Porterhouse over the telephone but needed confirmation now they were face-to-face.

'Is she dead you mean?'

Harry nodded.

'Oh yes. No doubt about that. Been dead an hour or two before anybody found her.'

'How?'

'This was what Porterhouse had refused to divulge over the phone.

'She was strangled.'

'Christ,' said Harry quietly.

'Yes. Somebody knocked her about a bit. There was a struggle, and then she was strangled.'

His mind pictured a hotel room with a body – the naked body of a woman – lying across the bed, but then backed off, refusing to contemplate the reality of it, what she must have suffered, her anguish and final despair. He felt a bitter anger that was partly at himself for not being in the office when she'd called but mostly at whoever had done that obscene thing to her and ended her life.

'And when . . . when did it happen?'

Porterhouse shrugged. 'Probably between four-thirty and five-thirty. We'll know for sure later on tonight.'

Later on tonight meant, of course, when they had the results of the post-mortem. He pictured her body on a slab, waiting to

129

be dissected, then again blotted it out.

'You say you were a friend of hers?' said Porterhouse, hitching up his trousers.

'Yes.'

'I gather she lived in Spain, is that right?'

'Yes.'

'So what had brought her back? Business, pleasure . . . what?'

'I don't know.'

'No? But she'd told you she was coming, hadn't she?'

'No.'

'Well, somebody had. I mean you knew she was here. You knew she was staying in this hotel.'

'She'd called at my office this afternoon. Only I wasn't there, and so she left a message.'

'Saying what?'

'Just letting me know she was here and giving me her phone number so I could ring her.'

Porterhouse stood regarding him. Perhaps not believing him. He didn't care. There was part of him felt he had helped connive at her death and so deserved to be suspected. He would have liked to confess, had he known for sure what he'd be confessing to.

'Who else might she have been seeing while she was over here?'

'I've no idea.'

'She never mentioned anybody else? Friends, family, anybody living in England?'

'I didn't know her for long.'

'How long?'

'Two weeks.'

'And how well?'

'I'm not sure.' Then, because he had to say it lest he be betraying her even on the day of her death, he said flatly, 'We were lovers.'

'I see,' said Porterhouse. 'Holiday romance, was it?' When Harry didn't reply, he added, 'So perhaps she was coming here to see you?'

130

'I wouldn't have thought so. I mean we didn't arrange . . . I didn't expect to see her again.'

Porterhouse remained lost in thought for a moment, then said, 'One minute', and left the office. There was a murmur of voices in conference. When Porterhouse returned, his manner was brisk.

'I'd like you to come along to the station. We can talk better there.'

Harry raised no objection. In any case, he wanted to be out of the hotel which had been the site of her death and was now full of those drawn there by it.

'The constable outside will take you. Have you got your own car here?' Harry nodded. 'Leave me the keys and I'll see it follows you.'

Handing over the keys, he felt he was relinquishing control over whatever might follow. He sat stupefied as a policeman drove him through London's familiar streets. They passed the Royal Albert Hall, where people were queuing for tickets. He wondered how much Porterhouse knew about Rebecca's association with Norris and about Norris's death. If he didn't know, then should he tell him? Was there a connection between the murderous assault on Rebecca and Norris's watery end?

Once inside the police-station, he thought to call Jill and tell her something of what had happened and to warn her he wouldn't be home for some time. There was a muttered debate between the policeman who'd been his driver and the desk-sergeant before he was given permission. It suggested he was a suspect, which came as no surprise. He suspected himself and so could expect no less from anyone else.

When he got through to Jill, it was a poor line.

'I'm going to be late home,' he said. 'Something's happened.'

'Where are you? I can hardly hear you.'

'I'm in a police-station.'

'A what?'

'Police-station. Rebecca Connors has been murdered.' There was no response, and he wondered whether the line had defeated him. 'Rebecca Connors has been murdered,' he repeated.

'Murdered . . . ?' said Jill, sounding as though she thought it was the line playing tricks.

'Murdered, yes,' he shouted back. 'Here, in a hotel in London.'

There was a pause; then she said, 'I'll see you later, then.'

Harry rang off and was shown into a small interview-room, which seemed identical to every other interview-room through which he'd passed in his chequered career. He was offered a cup of tea, which he accepted. Twenty minutes later Detective Inspector Porterhouse breezed in with the air of one to whom things were now becoming clearer. He perched on a chair across from Harry and rested his elbows on the table.

'Mr Sommers, did you know Norris Edgerton?'

'Yes.'

It was a reply that pleased him. 'I see. And you knew he was wanted for questioning regarding various serious offences committed in this country, did you?'

'Yes.'

'And you know he died just three or four weeks ago?'

'Yes.'

'And that this young lady whose body we've found today – this Rebecca Connors – she was his girl-friend?'

'Yes.'

Porterhouse gave a nod of satisfaction, then paused and scratched his head, as though not sure where all this rapid progress had taken him. He took out a packet of Benson and Hedges, lit one and offered one to Harry.

'No thanks.'

He exhaled a swirl of smoke. 'Do you think there is any connection between what's happened to this young lady today and what happened to her boy-friend a few weeks ago?'

'I don't know.'

'And what does that mean?'

'It means I don't know. I haven't the faintest bloody idea.'

'All right,' said Porterhouse, 'let's start again, shall we? From the beginning.'

'What beginning?'

'The holiday. Tell me all about it.'

Harry began not quite at the beginning, since instinct made him avoid mentioning Leo Shapiro's role in lending the villa. Otherwise he gave a faithful account of all that had led up to the party and then his own tentative enquiries that followed it.

'So you thought there was something fishy going on?' said Porterhouse.

'I wondered at first, but . . . everybody seemed to think it was an accident.'

'Did they, now?'

'Yes.'

He sensed that Porterhouse was as much adrift as himself, keeping him talking in the forlorn hope that something of significance would reveal itself. From time to time he would be called from the room. After one such absence he returned and said abruptly, 'You've got something of a record yourself, Mr Sommers.'

Harry nodded, not surprised he should have found this out. No doubt the police computer had done its stuff.

'Assault, wasn't it?'

Harry nodded again. No point in seeking to explain how life as a bouncer in London's clubland did occasionally land you in a tough spot where either you failed to defend yourself and got beaten up or you defended yourself effectively and got done for assault.

'And now here you are, all nice and respectable. Private detective. You know what I think? I think there should be a licensing system. Then people like you wouldn't get past the front door.' He was trying to work himself into a small rage, taking out his frustration.

'That charge of assault,' said Harry patiently, 'it wasn't on women.'

'I don't care who it was on. It still means you've got form. It means you're a man of violence. On women, on children, on grown men . . . I don't give a sod right now. What I want to know right now is – where were you between four and six o'clock?'

'Four o'clock I was talking to Mr Jessop.'

'And who's he when he's at home?'

'A solicitor.'

'I see. Very handy. And then?'

'There were three legal documents he wanted delivering to three people. I went to try and do this.'

'And did you?'

'I found two of them. The third I couldn't find, not yet.'

'And these two will confirm that, will they?'

Harry shrugged. 'I don't see why they shouldn't. My diary's in the car. Their names and addresses are in that. Or I suppose you could get them from Mr Jessop.'

But Porterhouse seemed already to be losing interest. 'I'm sure we could, yes.' He sat down and lit another cigarette. It was the signal for a further change of attitude to a more friendly approach. 'So tell me something.'

'What?'

'What do you think happened? I mean maybe she comes back to her room and there's somebody breaking in and she surprises them and they panic and end up killing her? Or is there a tie-up with this Norris Edgerton business?'

'Could be.'

'I know there could be. I want to know what you think.'

But he shook his head, refusing to be drawn. In truth, he didn't believe in the panicky burglar theory, not for a minute. His hunch was that Rebecca had died because of what had happened in Spain, but he couldn't quote rhyme or reason for it and so kept quiet.

He was kept hanging about for another half-hour, then given his car-keys and told he could go. His car he couldn't find at first. It wasn't at the front of the police-station but in the compound at the back. They must have searched it, he thought, opening the glove-compartment and checking that his diary and the undelivered legal document were still there, though whether they were just as he'd left them he couldn't have said.

It was gone midnight before he got back to the flat. There were lights on, which meant Jill was waiting up for him. In fact, she had fallen asleep on the sofa, with a pile of exercise-books on the floor beside her.

His entry disturbed her, and she shook herself awake. 'What time is it? Harry, are you all right?'

'Sure. The police wanted to see me, that's all.'

'What did they say?'

He felt reluctant to confide in her, knowing he couldn't do so fully and that any talk between them about Rebecca would be deceitful. Yet she was concerned and wanted to know all that had happened. He gave a brief, flavourless summary of the night's events.

'Poor Rebecca,' she said quietly. 'And why . . . ? I mean had she come over here for some specific reason?'

He looked at her and saw what she was wondering: whether Rebecca had come in search of him. It flashed through his mind that she might even suspect him of killing her.

'How the hell should I know?' he said roughly. 'She's dead. I haven't even seen her. Anyway, you look knackered. Why don't you get off to bed? I'm going to have a drink and unwind for a while.'

Seeing he didn't want her, she made no objection but rose and moved to the door. 'Good night, then.'

'Good night.'

He felt a curious relief as she went away into the bedroom. He closed the door and poured himself a large whisky. He couldn't sit but paced the room, needing to come to terms with this immobilising feeling of guilt. It was absurd to believe he should have been at the office when Rebecca had called there; he had had no way of expecting her; indeed, she'd spoken scornfully of London as the last place on earth she'd choose to be. As to whether he might have done more in Spain to satisfy her over Norris's death . . . that was surely wishful thinking and equally futile.

She had boasted to Yvonne about 'solving the mystery' of Norris's death. How? What more had she discovered? Presumably she'd been assisted by her tax lawyer boy-friend. Though how to find him would be another question.

Suppose, though . . . suppose the killer might now come looking for him? After all, while in Spain he'd conducted an investigation into Norris's death and done so on Rebecca's behalf. Then she'd called at his office in London only hours before meeting her own death. Whoever killed her had to consider the possibility that Harry knew as much as she did. If she were killed to keep her quiet, then it was only logical to regard himself as the next likely target. It was a prospect that gave him hope.

11.

The following morning it occurred to Harry he might not be the only one under threat from Rebecca's killer. He explained his fears to Jill over breakfast.

'Suppose Rebecca was killed to keep her mouth shut. Suppose she'd found out something about Norris's death and had come to England thinking she'd be safe here. Only somebody followed her and killed her because of what she knew.'

'Yes?' said Jill from over her copy of the *Guardian*.

'Well, anybody desperate enough to do that is desperate enough to kill again.'

'You mean you? That you might be in danger?'

'Or you.'

She stared in surprise. 'Me?'

'Well, all right, both of us. If there is some maniac looking for me because he thinks I might know whatever it was Rebecca knew . . . well, he might decide you must know it as well.'

She frowned. 'But we don't *know* that's why Rebecca was killed, do we?'

'No. I'm just saying *if*. If that's why, then because I was the one asking questions on her behalf and because we happen to live together . . . '

'Yes,' she said, cutting him short, 'I can see what you mean. But what do you suggest we do about it? Put some sort of announcement in the newspapers saying we honestly don't know anything so leave us alone please?'

'It's not funny,' he said quietly.

'I wasn't trying to be funny. Only I don't want any more playing at detectives. I don't want any more going on holiday and finding we're supposed to spend all our time with a gang of criminals. I just don't want any more to do with it, Harry.'

'No. I know you don't.'

'Well, then.'

'I'm just saying it might not be that easy. If whoever killed Rebecca killed her to keep her mouth shut . . . '

'Yes, I heard you the first time. Then they might decide they need to keep our mouths shut as well.'

'It's possible. That's all I'm saying – it's possible.'

'So what do you suggest we do about it?'

'Well, for one thing . . . '

'Yes?'

'I think perhaps you should move out of this flat.'

She hesitated only a moment, then nodded. 'OK.'

He hadn't expected such a prompt acquiescence. 'Well, I just think it's a sensible precaution . . . '

'Yes. I've said OK, I'll move out. Anything else?'

'Er . . . nothing specific. Just be on your guard. Try and vary the times of your regular journeys, make sure you don't always park your car in the same place . . . that sort of thing.'

'Right.'

'And for God's sake let me know if there's anybody asking about you or . . . well, anything out of the ordinary.'

'And that's as from now, is it? You don't want me to come back here tonight?'

'Yes,' he said, not sure it was quite what he intended but having to agree since he'd been the first to propose it.

'What about you? What will you do?'

'Oh, I'll probably stay here. I just don't want you to be in on your own, that's all.'

He was prepared for an argument, thinking she'd protest at his placing himself in the very danger he'd insisted she move away from. But she only said, 'Well, that's up to you', and returned to her newspaper.

Was she agreeing because she saw the undeniable sense of his proposal? Or was she simply seizing on it as an excuse to get away? He wondered whether, once out, she might not prefer it that way and refuse to move back in.

'I don't mean for very long,' he said.

'How long?'

'Oh . . . a week. Perhaps two.'

'Whatever you say.'

'Where will you go?'

'Oh, somebody at school will put me up. Probably Marcia. You remember Marcia? You met her at the sherry party.'

He nodded, remembering the petite, sari-clad maths-teacher who'd congratulated him on the beating-up of Jill's ex-husband. At least she sounded as though she might be on his side when the time came to persuade Jill to return.

'I don't actually think anything will happen,' he said. 'I daresay whoever killed her is miles away by now. But just in case. As a precaution.'

Yvonne, who read every newspaper she could get her hands on, already knew of Rebecca's death and needed only Harry's brusque confirmation that the victim was, indeed, the same attractive young lady who'd called to see him yesterday afternoon before she gave way to exclamations of horror and dismay.

'And she was so . . . well, she looked so healthy.'

'She was,' said Harry. 'Till somebody strangled her.'

'And have they any idea who did it?'

'I think I'm their number-one suspect at the moment.'

'Oh, but that's ridiculous. You couldn't have. I mean I know you didn't. But you couldn't have anyway, according to what the papers are saying about the time she was found.'

Harry let her go on, staring out through the reversed lettering on the window that said, 'Coronet Private Investigation Agency'. Beyond it was a street full of traffic and a world full of people indifferent to Rebecca's fate except as a piece of titillating journalism.

'If I give you some names,' he said, 'will you find out everything you can about them?'

'Well, yes,' she said, surprised. 'What names? And why?'

'Norris Edgerton,' he said, and waited for her to write it down.

She looked at him, realising now what he had in mind. 'But is it . . . ? I mean if the police are handling this, then surely . . . '

'Norris Edgerton,' he repeated.

She sighed, picked up a pencil and wrote. 'Yes.'

'Alan Mullins.'

'Who's he?' she asked, writing.

'Another of the gang we met in Spain. Let me just give you the names first, then I'll tell you all I know about 'em, and you can take it from there. Gerald Fieldhouse. Tommy Smith.' He was going to leave it at that but then, on impulse, added, 'Leo Shapiro.'

'Wasn't he one of our clients?'

'Yes. He also lent us the villa we stayed in.'

'I see,' said Yvonne. 'And what about the others?'

Harry gave her a brief run-down on what he knew of the other four, very brief in the case of Tommy Smith, about whom he knew virtually nothing save that he'd already disappeared before their holiday had begun. 'I know you haven't much to go on,' he said, 'but do what you can.'

'You're looking for something that might link them to this killing?'

He nodded. 'Or link them to one another in ways we don't already know.'

'It won't be easy,' she said, surveying the notes she'd taken.

He gave her an encouraging smile, knowing she was right but relying on the fact she was at her best when asked to do the near-impossible. She was a tenacious tracer and tracker-down of people, using her list of secret contacts – the DHSS, credit agencies, the police, newspaper libraries, priests, newsagents . . . most of whom even Harry wasn't allowed to know about. Some would do it for love, but the majority would require money, cash in hand or in discreet brown envelopes. The Agency's records would show only 'Petty cash, miscellaneous'.

'But suppose we do find something,' she asked, still with misgivings, 'we are going to pass it on to the police, aren't we?'

'Depends on what it is,' said Harry, who had no real plans, just a feeling he must do everything within his power.

140

She sighed. 'Well, it's up to you, of course. But the police aren't going to like it if they find out we've been withholding information.'

The police didn't even like the idea of a private agency taking initiatives of its own. Harry called at the Knightsbridge station to discover from Porterhouse what progress, if any, had been made. It went against the grain, this voluntary attendance where only last night he'd been taken as a suspect but it seemed the simplest way of finding out what he wanted to know.

In fact, Porterhouse had just arrived, looking depressed and hung-over. He observed Harry curiously, as if wondering whether he'd come to confess.

'And what can we do you for?' he asked, lighting a cigarette.

'I wondered if you'd come up with anything else since last night.'

'And why can't you wait to read about it in the papers like everybody else?'

'I knew her,' said Harry.

Porterhouse thought about it, then conceded, 'We've got the results of the post-mortem. I don't suppose there's any harm in me telling you that.'

'Thanks,' said Harry, trying to suppress the image, which mention of the post-mortem had re-awakened, of a naked and bloody Rebecca lying on a slab.

'Not that it told us much we didn't know already. Confirmed that time of death was between four and five in the afternoon. Cause of death was strangulation . . . ' As he spoke, he extracted a single sheet of typewritten paper from a pile on the corner of his desk and began to read from it. 'Bruising clearly evident on both sides of the neck . . . Fracture of the superior cornu of the thyroid . . . Abrasions on the lower lip and under the chin that would be consistent with efforts to loosen the grip . . . '

'Right, yes,' muttered Harry, having heard more than enough.

But Porterhouse hadn't finished: 'And, let's see, where are

we . . . ? Oh, yes. Examination of the vulva and hymen revealed no evidence of sexual assault or of forced penetration. Nor were any traces of seminal fluid found in the vagina.' Harry concentrated on the murky brown carpet at his feet, determined not to respond. Porterhouse allowed himself a small smile, then said. 'Anything else you want to know?'

Everything but that, thought Harry. 'What about . . . witnesses?'

'What witnesses? There weren't any.'

'No, but . . . wasn't anyone seen arriving or departing around the time of the murder?'

'Lots of people.'

'I mean anybody who seemed . . . '

'I know what you mean. And the answer's no. Nobody on reception can remember anybody acting suspicious or asking for Rebecca Connors's room number or anything of that sort. At least nobody we've talked to so far. We've still some hotel staff to see today. And guests for that matter. And there were no signs of a break-in, in case you want to know that as well. Looks like either her assailant used a key or else she opened the door and let him in.'

'You're sure that it was a him? I mean a male?'

'It would have had to have been a bloody big female. There's a bit I didn't read you in the post-mortem report about the positions of the thumb- and finger-prints. Suggests it was somebody with large hands. And, anyway, she wasn't some feeble geriatric, was she? She was a young, fit woman who put up quite a fight. I think we can safely assume it was a man, yes.'

It was a painful process, this circumstantial reconstruction of her death but, once started, he had to see it through.

'What about finger-prints?'

'Yes. On her throat. I've just told you.'

'I mean in the room . . . ?'

'One or two. Inside the wardrobe, inside drawers . . . places the cleaners hadn't bothered with. But so what? Don't forget this is a hotel room we're talking about. Used by lots of people who've put their sticky fingers all over it. I mean, all right, we

142

are trying to see who we can eliminate and what that leaves us with, but I can't see it getting us anywhere, if you want my opinion.'

'Did she make any phone-calls?' asked Harry.

Porterhouse stared at him and stubbed out his cigarette. 'Look, what is this? You think we're a load of wallies? You've come here to tell us how to do the job?'

'No. I just want to know what's happening.'

'Then read the bloody newspapers like everybody else.'

'I will. But I still want to know whether she made any phone-calls,' persisted Harry. 'Surely you can tell me that.'

'Jesus,' exclaimed Porterhouse. 'What is it with you? I mean, is this some sort of personal crusade or what?'

'I just want to know,' said Harry, forcing himself to speak quietly, both because he suspected it was the only way to get what he wanted and because if he ever began to lose an inch of control he didn't know where it would stop. 'And I was the last person she tried to see before she was killed.'

Porterhouse gave a groan of dismay. 'That makes you a suspect, not somebody who gets privileged treatment.'

'So I assume she did make some phone-calls,' said Harry. 'Since, if she didn't, you wouldn't mind telling me.'

'Oh, clever,' sneered Porterhouse. 'Very smart.'

'How many?'

Porterhouse rose from his desk, muttering, 'You've got a bloody nerve.' He opened a window, then came back and said flatly, 'Three. She made three calls, OK?'

'Who to?'

'We don't know. The rooms have direct dialling. All the hotel records show is how many calls and what they cost.'

'They don't record the numbers?'

'Unfortunately not. Some do. This particular hotel doesn't. Sorry.'

'Were any of them international calls?'

'No.'

'What about in-coming calls?'

'In-coming calls?'

'Yes.'

'You want to know about in-coming calls?'

'If possible.'

'Well, there, I'm afraid, with great sadness and many apologies . . . I can't help you.'

'You don't know?'

'I don't know. The hotel doesn't know. Nobody does. In-coming calls aren't recorded. They are simply put through. Now we've questioned the two telephonists who were on duty from the time Rebecca Connors signed into the hotel the previous evening to the time of her death, and neither of them have any recollection – I mean not any specific recollection one way or the other – of putting a call through to her. Now maybe you think I should have the two of 'em brought in for further questioning, or maybe you'd like to question them yourself . . . ?'

Harry let the sarcasm evaporate in the air between them, then said, 'Well, thanks anyway.'

'Oh, that's it, then, is it?'

'That's all I can think of for now, yes.'

'Well, I hope I've been of some assistance. Now what about you?'

'What?'

'What about you being of some bloody assistance? What about you telling me everything you know? I mean everything this time.'

'I already have—' Harry began to protest.

'Bullshit.'

'I don't know who killed her.'

'No?'

'No.'

'Do you know anybody who might know who killed her?'

Yes, he did, he realised. But he wasn't going to give Porterhouse the pleasure of talking to him, not till he'd done so himself.

'No.'

Porterhouse gave a grunt of dismay and scratched his head. Then he stood up, hitched up his trousers and wandered over to the window. 'So why are you in here this morning, asking me all these questions?'

'Because I want to know what's going on.'

'You do.'

'Yes.'

'OK. But let me warn you, Mr Private Eye. I don't want any smart aleck thinking he can teach me my job, savee?'

'Sure,' said Harry.

'So don't get any bright ideas about solving this yourself. Just let me catch you trying and I'll do you for wasting police time. Which, now I come to think about it, is what you're doing now. So just fuck off out of it, will you, and don't let me see you back inside this building unless it's because I've sent for you.'

He managed to apply himself to the routine tasks of the day, though a copy of the *Evening Standard* caught him by surprise. Leafing through it over a lunch-time sandwich, he was suddenly face-to-face with a picture of Rebecca. A younger Rebecca certainly, with a page-boy bob and a halter-neck dress – but unmistakably her. The story that went with the picture was headlined, 'Murdered Blonde in Hotel Bedroom', and gave the basic facts of the case as Harry already knew them. He turned over to the sports pages but found it difficult to concentrate and ended by throwing the paper away along with what was left of his sandwich.

When he returned to the office, there was a message for him from Jill.

'She said to tell you she's arranged to stay with Marcia,' relayed Yvonne. 'This is the address and the phone number' – handing him a piece of paper – 'and she says sleep well and she hopes to see you soon.'

'Thanks,' said Harry.

'I gather you thought it might be dangerous for her to stay in the flat.'

'Well . . . just for the time being, yes.' Jill's de-camping was already beginning to feel like an over-reaction on both their parts. He had offered it as a suggestion for debate, but, with a speed that left no opportunity for either debate or second thoughts, she'd gone like a shot.

He hadn't forgotten Porterhouse's question – 'Do you know anybody who might know who killed her?' – and, his day's work completed, he headed south, across the river. It was half-six by the time he came to the New Oasis Club where, by the look of it, business had just about begun. There was a new face in the box office, an unkempt, middle-aged man who stared at him through runny eyes.

'Shapiro in?' Harry asked.

'You what? Are you a member?'

'Yes,' said Harry. 'Life member.' And walked on past him and into the club, ignoring the cry of 'Hey, hang on a minute . . . !' that followed him. There were only a couple of customers, sitting at separate tables. Dave was behind the bar and gave Harry an almost imperceptible nod of recognition.

'Shapiro in?' repeated Harry.

'Yes.'

Without waiting for further invitation, Harry went through the door beside the bar. Dave watched him go, expressionless. He went down the corridor and to the open door of Shapiro's office. Shapiro was at his desk and looked up, startled. He had a biro in his hand and, on his desk, a pocket calculator and account book. Through the window that gave a view into the porno cinema Harry caught a glimpse of a naked woman, three times larger than life, covering herself in shampoo.

'Harry, well . . . !' Shapiro began, recovering.

'Save it.' Harry leant on the desk and looked down at the face with its frozen, uncertain smile. 'You're glad to see me, I know. I've heard it all before. Now tell me everything you know about Rebecca Connors.'

'Who?' It was a good attempt but not quite convincing.

'You know who.'

'Oh, the girl . . . ?'

'The girl.'

'I read about it, yes . . . '

146

'I'm sure you did. Now what do you know about it? Who killed her?'

Shapiro attempted a laugh. 'Jesus, Harry, who do you think I am that I'm going to know things like that? I mean, come on . . .'

'You're well-informed, Leo. You like to keep well-informed so you don't get any nasty surprises. Remember telling me that?'

'Yes, but not . . . Look, sit down. Let's talk about this in a civilised fashion.'

'Who?' insisted Harry, bringing his fist down on the desk so that the pocket calculator jumped.

'I don't know who. How the hell am I supposed to know . . . ?' He broke off as his look went past Harry to the doorway. Harry turned and saw that Dave had appeared, either summoned by some signal from Shapiro or simply alerted by the raised voices. 'Now, Harry,' said Shapiro, regaining his confidence, 'like I said, if you want to talk, we can talk in a civilised fashion. If you don't, then I'm going to have to ask Dave here to show you the door.'

'I wouldn't do that,' said Harry, who suddenly felt like thumping somebody and didn't much care who.

'Dave,' said Shapiro with a nod which meant go ahead and throw him out.

As Dave took an obedient step forward, Harry threw a left hook, high from his shoulder, that caught Dave unprepared and rocked him back. He gave a grunt of surprise, then lunged forward with both arms flailing. Harry took a couple of blows, one on his forearm, the other to the side of his head, as he attempted to avoid the wild swings and found himself jammed against the desk. Then he got in a short, solid punch to the stomach that stopped the other man's rush and allowed him to move away so that he didn't have Shapiro and the desk behind him.

'Throw him out,' yelled Shapiro, who'd backed away into the far corner. 'Go on.'

Dave looked at him and then looked at Harry, as if not sure

147

any more who was the real enemy of the two. 'Look, what the fuck is this?' he said, gasping for breath. 'What're you after?'

'I'm after what he knows,' said Harry.

Dave turned to Shapiro. 'What?'

'Never mind what. I want him out of here!'

'You heard him,' said Dave apologetically. 'Me, I don't know what the fuck this is about, but if he says he wants you out then I've got to ask you to go.'

'There was a woman killed yesterday,' said Harry. 'And I think your boss knows more about it than he's letting on.'

'What woman?'

'Rebecca Connors.'

Dave shook his head; the name meant nothing. 'Round here, was it?'

'No. Hotel up in Knightsbridge.'

'Look, I know nothing about it,' protested Shapiro. 'I swear on the lives of my wife and kids. Nothing. Now throw him out, will you!'

'You heard him,' said Dave, with a shrug that suggested he didn't believe Shapiro either.

Harry suddenly felt defeated. Not by Dave and his strong-arm tactics. He just knew there was no way he'd be able to shake Shapiro, now he was on his guard and over the initial shock. Whatever he made him confess to, he'd never know whether it was the truth or lies and so would be no nearer his goal.

'Don't worry. I'm going,' he said to Dave, who looked relieved.

That night, alone in the flat, he tried to assess what little he knew. For a start, just how many murders had actually occurred? Rebecca had been strangled, no doubt about that, with the pressure marks on her neck testifying to the murderous intent of her assailant. Norris's death was more ambiguous. The Spanish police had declared it an accident, as had the doctor who had attended the scene. Then there was Tommy Smith's empty villa and the dust-covered Merc standing outside it,

148

which could mean anything.

Was he again letting his emotions run away with him in believing he might succeed in unravelling all this where the police couldn't? They had all the advantages of authority and resources. He had only one: he'd known Rebecca alive where they hadn't. She'd called him on the morning of their departure from Spain to tell him how Norris had been withdrawing large amounts of cash prior to his death. Did that mean he was being blackmailed? For what and by whom?

The more he thought about it, the less sure he was whether he held all the pieces of a jigsaw that needed only re-arranging to reveal its true picture or whether there was no complete picture after all. Perhaps Norris's death had been due to accidental drowning, Rebecca had surprised a hotel burglar and Tommy Smith was even now living it up in Costa Rica.

The thing he did know for certain was that the flat felt desolate without Jill. What had happened at the New Oasis, when he'd used his fists to deal with the hapless Dave, had been a danger sign of how, without her, he might so easily regress to the street fighter he'd been before she came along. The prospect of assault from Rebecca's killer seemed less alarming than the prospect of Jill deciding to stay where she was and sending round a van to collect her belongings.

12.

Porterhouse rang Harry at the office three days later.

'I don't know why I'm telling you this,' he said, 'but Rebecca Connors is being buried at Henley-on-Thames tomorrow morning, eleven o'clock. Apparently that's where her family live.'

'Thanks,' said Harry, who hadn't until this moment even thought of her funeral or whether he would attend but now decided instantly that he would. 'Any progress on finding out who killed her?'

'If there is you'll read about it in the newspapers like everybody else,' said Porterhouse, and he rang off.

Next morning was warm and had a smell of Spring about it. Bunches of crocuses had sprung from the tubs Jill had set beside the back door. Harry set out in good time, knowing he had to cross London and not knowing how difficult it might be to find the cemetery at Henley-on-Thames. In the event he travelled quickly, going in the opposite direction to the heaviest of the traffic, and spotted the cemetery within five minutes of arriving. It was laid out on a hill-side, overlooking the river. He parked his car before the gates and went in.

There was a small chapel, complete with spire and bell and florid stained glass, but it was locked and deserted, making him wonder whether the ceremony was taking place elsewhere before the body was brought here or whether he was in the wrong place altogether. He walked among the tomb-stones, reading the names and dates and the inscriptions which the older ones bore, proclaiming, 'An Angel Returned To Her Maker' and 'May Perpetual Light Shine Upon Him'. Between the graves the grass had begun to grow, producing a lush, blowsy effect at odds with the uniformed rows.

At the end of one such row he came to a newly dug grave

which gaped open and had planks laid so as to form platforms along each side. Perhaps this was for her, he thought, looking down into it.

Going back towards his car, he met a man arriving by bicycle, whose weather-tanned face and rough clothes suggested he was there to work rather than to visit. Harry stopped him and asked if he knew if there was a burial due for eleven o'clock. He was assured that there was, yes. The man produced from his pocket a grubby document which bore the name of the deceased – 'Rebecca Connors'. Harry returned to his car to wait for the cortège.

It was eleven-fifteen before the first of three black limousines came past him and turned in at the cemetery gates. They were followed by two other cars, in one of which he recognised Porterhouse with a police driver. He left his own car and hurried after them.

The procession stopped as close to the newly dug grave as the road would take it, and there was an opening of car doors as the mourners emerged, eight of them altogether. The third limousine carried a clergyman in his black-and-white garb and two choir-boys with unlit candles. It was this vicar who gave the lead, striding purposefully towards the graveside. Behind him, the mourners clutched one another's arms and followed, and the undertakers unloaded the coffin on to a trolley that ran easily across the grass. There were few wreaths. Harry silently rebuked himself for not having thought to send one. He passed Porterhouse, who gave a nod from inside his car, and went to stand a discreet distance from the other mourners. One or two gave him curious glances but said nothing.

The vicar began to pray, blessing the coffin with a sprinkler of holy water. The two choir-boys chanted the responses to the prayers while the other mourners mumbled along at the more familiar phrases. Harry supposed that the middle-aged couple standing arm-in-arm beside the vicar were Rebecca's parents; and there was a blonde girl with glasses who might have been a younger sister. Finally the prayers were over, and the coffin was lowered. One of the undertakers held a silver scoop of earth from which he invited the mourners to take a handful and scatter it on the coffin. Harry declined and went back to his car.

He thought of Rebecca luxuriating in the heat of Spain, barefoot and wearing her Hertz Rent-A-Car tee-shirt. Now here she was, being laid to rest with a view of the Thames and a ceremony that was a model of Anglican restraint. She would have hated it.

'How was it?' asked Yvonne cheerily when he got back to the office.

'All right as funerals go. I'm glad I went, let's put it that way.'

He had had his doubts, wondering what he was doing hovering uninvited on the fringes of a funeral from which, he was sure, Rebecca would have expressly barred him, had she had the chance. Then he had stopped for a pint on his way back and realised he was glad he'd been there to say goodbye.

'They always say funerals are a help, don't they?' went on Yvonne. 'To the living I mean. I can't suppose they do much for the dead.'

'I don't suppose they do,' he agreed absent-mindedly, pouring himself a cup of tea. What, he wondered, had Porterhouse been doing there? Had he really been hoping to spot an unexpected face among the few mourners, the face of her murderer? Or was he, like Harry, present because he felt a debt to her, the need to apologise for not having come up with her killer?

'How's Jill?' asked Yvonne.

'Jill . . . ?'

'Is she still with her friend or have you thought it safe for her to move back into the flat yet?'

Harry looked at her but could tell nothing from those owlish eyes that stared back in apparent innocence. Once he would have taken the question at face value, a polite show of concern. Now, knowing her better, he suspected she was aware of the untoward haste with which Jill had moved out and was wondering, as he was, when she would ever move back in again.

'She's been busy,' he said abruptly. 'I haven't seen her for a day or two.'

'You'll be looking forward to having her back, though, I suppose?'

'Yes.' Then, wanting to change the subject: 'What about those names I gave you? Are you getting anywhere with 'em?'

She sighed. 'Oh yes. I was wanting to talk to you about that.'

'Go on, then.'

'Well, it's proving very difficult. I mean *very* difficult.'

'Why?'

'Well, they're not exactly your leading citizens, are they? I mean they're either your out-and-out criminals or the next thing to it.'

Harry nodded. 'Definitely.'

'So either they've got a criminal record – which you know about already – or they've been very careful not to get one, in which case nobody seems to have heard of 'em.'

'So what have you got?' said Harry. 'What about Norris Edgerton?'

Yvonne consulted her notes. 'Norris Edgerton. Born 1940 . . .'

'And died three weeks ago.'

'Pardon?'

'Nothing. Go on.'

'Born 1940. Did a spell in Borstal when he was seventeen. So that would be, what, '57. Then he was convicted of burglary in 1962, for which he served six months. And I haven't been able to find anything on him since then, not a thing, except what you've told me.' She looked up at him. 'The trouble is, with him going to live in Spain and then dying there and everything, Scotland Yard have taken an interest and so it's all that much more difficult to get access to his record. Once they're involved, he becomes an RAO. That means Restricted Access Only. It also means that none of our normal contacts can get a look at it. Well, not without having to declare their interest, which, of course, they're not too keen on doing.'

'I see. So what about the others?'

She returned to her notes. 'Well, the next name you gave me

was Alan Mullins. He also has a prison record. He served three years from 1978 to 1981 for theft and aggravated burglary. And he's not very popular with the credit agencies. He's listed as a bad debtor by more than one. The only other thing I could find out was that he used to be a member of the Bermuda Blues.'

'The what?'

'Some sort of pop group. They released a record in 1974, but it didn't get anywhere. And that's about it. Oh, I mentioned what you'd told me about that raid on the jeweller's in Bond Street and, although nobody would commit themselves, I'm sure you're right that he was involved. It's just that, like I say, now Scotland Yard have shown an interest, there's a limit to what our usual sources can find out.'

Her repeated references to Scotland Yard and the interest they were taking made him wonder. 'What is all this about the Yard anyway? Why should they be so keen all of a sudden?'

'Well, I don't suppose it is all of a sudden, is it? I mean they must have been keeping an eye on these people ever since they fled to Spain. And now, with what's happened in the last few weeks, they're bound to be interested.'

'I suppose so.' He remembered what Doctor Natras had told him about the two detectives who'd flown over to check on Norris's identity. 'But do you get the impression they think there's something more to all this?'

'More than what?'

She could be obstinately unhelpful when she wanted to be. He sighed and said patiently, 'More than an accidental death in Spain, followed by the unrelated murder of a young woman in a London hotel room.'

'I don't know. I suppose they have to keep an open mind, don't they?'

He thought of Porterhouse, whose mind seemed not only open but fairly empty. 'Yes, but do they think the two deaths might be connected?'

'I don't know,' said Yvonne firmly. 'The only contacts I have are with civilian admin staff and local CID. They're people who have access to what's on general record but not to what

Scotland Yard might be thinking.'

'All right,' he said, giving up. 'So what about the others? Gerald Fieldhouse. What about him?'

This time she made a show of re-reading her notes before replying. It was a small protest against his persistent questions. Only when she had made him wait did she say, 'Oh yes, here we are.'

'Good,' muttered Harry.

'Gerald Fieldhouse. Born 1947. Yes, he's got quite a record, has Mr Fieldhouse.' Then she thought of a joke. 'I don't mean he was also a member of the Bermuda Blues. This is a different type of record I'm talking about.' Harry rewarded her with a smile, and she continued: 'He was in and out of court as a juvenile, but if we stick to the serious stuff then he has convictions for assault, burglary and grievous bodily harm. He seems to have been rather a wild sort of character.'

And hasn't changed, thought Harry, remembering his enthusiastic beating-up of the motorbike youths who'd pinched Jill's handbag and his frequent outbursts against Samantha.

'Do you want all the gruesome details?' she asked.

'Not particularly. Is there anything that ties him to any of the other names I gave you?'

'No,' she said, and she looked at him with pursed lips as if defying him to challenge her judgement.

He just nodded and said, 'Anything else?'

'Only that his wife's suing him for divorce on the grounds of desertion.'

'I can't say I blame her.'

'I've got her name and address if you want it.'

Not really, he thought, but knew better than to throw the results of Yvonne's diligent research back in her face. 'Thanks,' he said, and took the piece of paper she handed him.

'By the way, that's his second marriage.'

'Yes?'

'He got divorced from his first wife seven years ago, and then two years later she took out a court order for non-payment of maintenance.'

155

'I don't suppose she's had much joy with that.'

'I don't think so, no.'

It helped to explain why, of all the villains, Fieldhouse had been the happiest with his exile. He was escaping not only the law but two wives, both out for his blood. Even given a Royal Pardon he might well have elected to stay where he was. Harry wondered how much of this was known to Samantha. Probably none of it. And certainly none of it seemed remotely relevant to what had subsequently happened to Norris and Rebecca.

'Anything else?'

'Not on him, no.'

'Tommy Smith, then?'

She turned over to a new page. 'He was born in Brighton in 1941, served in the army 1959 to '60, then ended up in prison in 1962, serving six months for burglary.'

Harry stared. '1962?'

'The same year as Norris Edgerton,' she said, anticipating his question. 'Not all that surprising, since they were sentenced together. They'd raided a sub-post office in Lewisham.'

Rebecca had once said that Norris and Tommy Smith went back a long way, and now here was the proof of it. It also established the beginnings of Norris's fascination with sub-post offices as soft targets where robbery was concerned.

'And what happened to him after that?' asked Harry.

'Well, apparently he ran a mini-cab firm for quite a few years. Then in 1969 he was prosecuted for receiving but was found not guilty. Six months later he was in court again, this time charged with intimidating witnesses.'

'These were the witnesses at his first trial, were they?'

'I don't know. I wouldn't be surprised, though.'

'Neither would I. And what happened?'

'He was found not guilty again.'

'So, if he was intimidating witnesses, he must have been bloody good at it.'

'Looks like it.'

'Go on.'

'Well, there isn't much more. He was married in 1973, but his

156

wife was killed four years later in a car accident.'

'What sort of car accident?'

'I don't know. I only know what it said on her death certificate. Multiple injuries following motor accident.'

'Yes, OK,' muttered Harry. It wouldn't help to insist on suspecting every event in the past lives of these people. Even the wives of villains could be the innocent victims of road accidents.

'How did he end up in Spain?' he asked.

'Apparently he was involved in a big antiques robbery. Hundreds of thousands of pounds' worth. He was arrested and charged but then escaped before the case could come to court.'

'Escaped . . . ?'

She shrugged. 'Don't ask me how. All I was told is that he escaped from custody. And the next anyone heard of him was when he popped up in Spain, where they couldn't touch him.'

'I see. And what about his most recent disappearance? Are Scotland Yard interested at all?'

'I've no idea. I assume they think he's still living over there.'

'Oh.'

'Perhaps you should tell them he's gone missing.'

Perhaps he should. Or perhaps he'd just give himself a little more time to see if he could make head or tail of the whole business before going back to Porterhouse and saying, all right, I give up and here are one or two facts I didn't get around to mentioning when we spoke before. And then explain about Norris's cash withdrawals and Tommy Smith's mysterious absence. After which he would no doubt get a bollocking for withholding information.

'So,' he said, 'the one and only common denominator we've come across so far is that Norris Edgerton and Tommy Smith were both involved in a sub-post office job in the early sixties. For which they both did time.' Even as he spoke, it sounded futile. A single straw which wouldn't support even the lightest of drowning men.

'I suppose it is,' Yvonne agreed.

'Anything else?'

157

'About Tommy Smith?'

'Yes.'

'No.'

Which left just one name from his original list. Curiously, it was the name of a person he had least reason to suspect – who hadn't really been part of Norris's gang, who didn't seem to have any motive and who was punctilious about keeping his own nose clean – yet who he couldn't help thinking might just know more than all the rest put together.

'Leo Shapiro, then,' he said.

Her expression wasn't encouraging. 'Well, isn't he a friend of yours anyway?'

'No,' said Harry, under no qualms about that any more. 'He's an acquaintance, somebody I happen to know.'

'But he lent you his villa.'

'He also tried to have his bouncer beat me up.'

'Really?' she said, astonished.

'Yes. So forget the friendship idea. If he's got to be something then he's an enemy, OK?'

'Whatever you like. But what I mean is you probably know more about him already than I've been able to find out.'

'And what's that?' said Harry stubbornly.

She looked again at her pad. 'Leo Emmanual Shapiro,' she recited flatly. 'Born 1948. Married 1972. Together with Mrs Shapiro, he owns Shapiro Properties Limited and Shapiro Developments Limited and Shapiro Management Limited.' She stopped.

'And that's it?'

'That's it. I warned you there wasn't much. Oh yes, and he pays his bills promptly.'

'You mean he paid us for the job we did?'

'Exactly.'

'Well, he knew everybody else on that list,' mused Harry aloud. 'There's a picture in the bedroom of his villa to prove it.'

'That's as may be. But he's got no criminal record. At least not one I could find.'

158

'I'm sure he hasn't. He's too careful, and he's got too much money.'

Yvonne waited a moment, then said, 'I did add one more name to your list if you'd like to hear about him.'

'What name?' said Harry, surprised.

'Eric Buller.'

It took a moment to place it. 'The man Shapiro wanted us to trace . . . ?'

'Yes. It's just I thought if I was supposed to be finding out everything I could about Shapiro then at least that was one lead we had already. And since I didn't find many more to follow up, I made a few enquiries about him.'

'And did you get anywhere?' asked Harry, intrigued. He remembered his trek to Slough and how he'd wondered at the time what misfortune could have befallen Eric Buller to have brought him from the suburban splendours of Dulwich to the miserable terrace in which he'd found him. Nor had he ever understood why Shapiro had been so anxious to re-establish contact with his ex-neighbour.

'Well, I don't know,' said Yvonne. 'That's up to you to decide.'

But there was now something teasing in her manner, a hint that here at last she had something worth reporting.

'So what did you find?' he asked, trying not to sound impatient.

'Well, I don't know why your Mr Shapiro wanted to get in touch with him.'

'Oh,' said Harry, disappointed.

'But I do know why he moved house and everything. I mean there was a specific reason. It wasn't just that he preferred the area.'

'I'm sure it wasn't,' said Harry. 'So what was it?'

When she told him, he was again disappointed. It hardly seemed the missing link for which he was forlornly searching. Just a sad tale of greed and foolishness that had ruined Eric Buller's comfortable life for him but appeared to offer Harry no help in his quest.

159

Till he thought some more about it and then began to wonder.

Taking the morning off to attend Rebecca's funeral had left his afternoon even busier than usual so that it stretched into the early evening. Though this was a blessing in disguise with Jill still absent from the flat. He was in no hurry to return to its silent rooms and so stopped off at an Italian restaurant close to the office for a plateful of cannelloni, washed down by a bottle of red wine.

It also gave him the opportunity to consider further what he'd heard from Yvonne on the subject of Eric Buller.

He was in no doubt that what she had told him was true. She always enjoyed her small triumphs when, like a conjuror producing rabbits, she would pull some unexpected piece of information from her hat. And what she had told him made immediate sense of Eric Buller's dramatically reduced circumstances.

But did it help make sense of anything else? That is, of Norris's Spanish tragedy and the even more tragic aftermath that had taken place in Majors Hotel, Knightsbridge? There were several ways to try and find out. Harry decided on the most direct, declined the offer of the sweet trolley, swilled down the last of his wine and set off along the M4 towards Slough.

It was going dark by the time he found Caledonian Road again, though at least this time the weather was fine and without the chilling wind that had accompanied his first visit. The road itself didn't seem to have changed much. If the dustbins had been emptied at all, they had been instantly re-filled to overflowing. The abandoned-looking house had been boarded up, so that there were now two on the row with sheets of hardboard instead of doors and windows.

The front door of number 58 still had neither bell nor knocker. Harry rapped on it and had to wait no more than a moment before it was opened by Mrs Buller. Her appearance was as immaculate as last time. Though, if her make-up and expensive woollen suit suggested she was prepared for the arrival of visitors, her manner, defensive and hostile, suggested they seldom arrived.

'Yes?'

'My name's Harry Sommers. I came to see your husband some weeks ago . . . '

'Oh yes,' she said, recognising him. 'What is it now?'

'I'd like to see him again.'

'Why?'

'Well, I'd like to talk to him about that. Is he at home?'

He thought for a moment she was going to say no, that he'd gone away leaving her with not the slightest idea when he'd ever be back. Then she gave a shrug of indifference and said, 'Yes. Come on in.'

She turned and went down the hallway, leaving him to close the front door and follow her. At least now he understood her attitude more than he had previously and so found it easier to forgive. They entered the same room, crowded with furniture and dominated by the television-set on which the news was being shown. The pekinese dog, spread before the empty grate of the fireplace, looked round and gave a petulant yelp at Harry's appearance.

'Somebody to see you,' Mrs Buller announced in a voice tinged with disbelief, as though she found the very idea faintly ridiculous.

Eric Buller looked at Harry in surprise. He was sitting in his armchair, with a bottle of whisky and a glass at his elbow.

'Oh,' he said, and then, as recognition came to him, 'Oh. Hello.'

'Harry Sommers,' said Harry. 'I came to see you a few weeks ago . . . '

'Oh yes, I remember. Come in and sit down.'

His wife bent and scooped up the pekinese to her bosom. 'We'll leave you to your discussions,' she said.

'Thank you, dear,' said Eric Buller with a sly smile.

She shot him a suspicious glance, the pekinese hissed through its tiny teeth, and the pair of them left the room.

161

'Well, this is a surprise,' said Eric Buller. 'A pleasant one I must admit.'

'Is it?'

'Oh yes. Your last visit was most profitable. And enjoyable. Got me out of this hole for a while, which is always something I'm grateful for. Would you like a drink?'

'Yes,' said Harry. 'I don't mind if I do.'

Eric Buller raised himself from his armchair, took another glass from the sideboard and poured a generous measure from the whisky bottle. 'Your very good health.'

'Cheers,' said Harry.

He settled back into his chair. 'So, to what do we owe the pleasure this time?'

'Do you mind if I close the door?' said Harry.

Buller looked surprised, but didn't object. 'No. No, you go ahead.'

'And could we have the telly off?'

'Certainly.'

He was raising himself from his chair to reach for it, but Harry was there first and switched it off. Buller eyed him warily as if beginning to wonder what all this was about.

Harry smiled. 'Now we can talk.'

'Yes,' said Buller, shifting uneasily. 'But what exactly . . . I mean, just what is it you want to talk about?'

'Well, I suppose you could call this a de-briefing session.'

'A what?'

'Leo asked me to call and check that everything went to plan.'

There was a pause, then Buller said, 'But I've already spoken to him on the phone. I rang him the day I got back.'

Harry smiled again. 'Oh, I'm sure you did. But you know Leo. He doesn't like leaving anything to chance. Always likes to be sure. And even then, when he's sure, he wants everything double-checking.' Buller nodded, but Harry could see the doubt was still there in his eyes and so he took a gamble and said, 'Look, I don't mind if you want to ring him now and check for yourself that all this is above board.'

Buller hesitated. Don't you dare take me up on it, you

bastard, thought Harry, looking him in the eye.

'Er, no . . . no, I'm sure that won't be necessary,' said Buller, who might have come down in the world but still kept his middle-class sensibilities that didn't allow him to call the other man a liar to his face.

'Well, then,' said Harry, 'perhaps it'd be simplest if you told me everything that happened after I last called to see you.'

The account Buller gave was disarmingly frank and, repeated in a court of law, would have earned him a considerable prison sentence. Harry fought to disguise his own surprise and the turmoil of emotions the revelations provoked. Having struggled for so long to make sense of events that had remained obstinately baffling, it was breath-taking to have the whole solution suddenly laid out before him.

'Thank you,' he said, when Buller had finished.

'And that's it, then, is it?'

'Yes, I think that's all. Sorry to have troubled you.'

'No trouble. Glad I could help. Just so long as that miserable old bitch through there doesn't find out what I've been up to.'

Harry let himself out of the house. It was now dark, but he felt as though a great and shining light had been shed upon the world. He drove slowly back into London, contemplating his next move. He had set out to avenge Rebecca's murder without knowing how or where it would take him. Now he knew all about Tommy Smith and Norris and therefore why Rebecca had been killed. He also knew about Leo Shapiro's involvement, though that no longer seemed so important. All that mattered now was to find the murderer and bring him to some sort of justice, rough or otherwise.

13.

The next day, a Saturday, was the opening of the cricket season. For Harry it was a day to be spent, more dangerously, in pursuit of a man he believed to be a killer. He went out to the car for his road atlas, coming back indoors to find the telephone ringing.

He picked up the receiver. 'Hello?'

It was Jill, sounding brisk and determined, as though facing up to a difficult task. 'Harry, it's me. I thought I'd come round today and wanted to know when I'd catch you in.'

It was a call he wasn't prepared for; his mind was elsewhere. 'What, you're, er . . . you're moving back in?'

'Well . . . it's not as simple as that. I want us to talk.'

'What about?'

'No, not over the phone. I can't talk to you like this. That's why I want to know when you'll be in.'

'Well, not this morning,' he said, at a loss. He knew he should be alarmed by this rather formal request for the meeting, as though he were a parent of one of her pupils, but his present task preoccupied him. There would be a time for Jill later, when the other thing was over.

'Well, this afternoon, then?' she said, becoming exasperated.

'I don't know.'

'Well, when? What's the matter?'

'All right, this afternoon,' he said. 'But I don't know what time.'

'Don't worry. I'll wait,' she said angrily, and rang off.

He opened the road atlas and found the page which featured London and the Home Counties. As he'd expected, his best route was along the M4, a virtual re-run of his trip to Slough, coming off at junction six, though this time heading south through Windsor and Eton, then on to one of the minor roads that would take him to Palmer's Heath.

It was a picturesque jumble of pub and Norman church and houses of dressed stone, this place chosen by Norris Edgerton for his retirement. There was a village green, with 'No Parking' signs, and a small pond bereft of ducks. Only the south edge of the village had been allowed to spread into council houses, a garage with garish flags flying and a small plastics factory.

The pub was called the Rose and Crown and had mullioned windows. Harry parked on the pub car-park, though for once he was in search of information rather than liquid refreshment. In fact, the doors to the saloon bar were still locked and bolted. He had to wait ten minutes before gaining admission to a room full of pewter and horse-brasses. The landlord who admitted him had a thick, black beard and ruddy features.

'Not a bad morning,' he said, going back to behind his bar where he was sorting money into the till.

'Not bad at all,' agreed Harry.

'You look like you've been catching the sun.'

'I've been abroad. Spain.' He ordered a half of bitter, then asked, 'You don't happen to know a Mrs Edgerton who lives round here, do you?'

The landlord scratched his beard and pondered. 'Can't say as I do,' he pronounced finally, placing the drink on the bar. 'Thirty-eight, if you please.'

'Have you got a telephone directory I could look at?'

'Certainly.'

He disappeared for a moment, then returned with a directory, which he plonked down on the bar, scooping up the thirty-eight pence worth of change Harry had put there.

'Cheers,' said Harry, and he carried the directory and his drink to one of the low wooden tables. He leafed through the 'E's and found a small column of eight or nine Edgertons. The first was a doctor and the second a butcher and could be ignored, but the third – 'Edgerton, L., 8 Saxon Close, Palmer's Heath' – was much more encouraging. He recalled Shapiro referring to Mrs Edgerton as 'Lesley': 'She's a tough cookie, is

Lesley. She'll get over it,' he had said when Harry had gone to the New Oasis Club to return the keys of the villa. What's more, the single initial, 'L', suggested somebody living alone; since the full name hadn't been given, more likely a woman than a man.

Harry returned to the bar with his empty glass and the directory. 'Where will I find Saxon Close?' he asked.

'Saxon Close . . . ?' The landlord scratched his beard again, but this time nodded. 'You're in a car, are you?'

'Yes.'

'Then you should have no problems. You go right out of here. Follow the road as far as the Grange. Now you can't miss that. That's a great big house with a row of four chimney-pots. And, anyway, they're having a fête there today, so it's full of tents and what-not. You go past there, take the first on your left, and Saxon Close is about another half-mile.'

'Thanks,' said Harry.

'Mind, if it's anybody from round here you're wanting, they're as likely as not to be at this fête I'm telling you about. Starts around midday I believe.'

Outside, things had become busier – people bustling to the shops or walking their dogs. But still it remained an English backwater where not much ever happened, save for today when there was the annual fête at the Grange and, if Harry was right, a murderer on the loose.

He drove off, following the directions given him by the landlord. The Grange was, indeed, difficult to miss: a square, Georgian house with the imposing row of promised chimney-pots. It was surrounded by a large and carefully tended garden, which, in turn, was surrounded by iron railings. Among its trees people were arranging stalls and putting up hand-drawn posters.

He took the next turning left and soon came upon Saxon Close, a row of hunched cottages that might once have been where farm labourers lived but now had been up-graded and had a Volvo and a BMW standing outside them. Harry slowed, took them in at a glance and then carried on up the road since there was no obvious place to stop without being conspicuous. It was some distance along the road before he was able to turn and come back again, this time more cautiously, knowing what to expect. He stopped short of the cottages and on a slight rise so that he overlooked them. He counted eight separate dwellings, which made it a toss-up whether number 8 was the nearest or the furthest away. He decided to wait and see what happened.

For the next half-hour very little did. A man in a straw hat emerged from one of the cottages which was in the middle of the row, and therefore clearly not number 8, and began to mow the small rectangle of grass before it. Then a youngish couple came out from the cottage next-door and got into the BMW, calling a greeting to their neighbour before they drove away, heading into Palmer's Heath.

Harry resolved to give it another half-hour and then, when that had elapsed without further event, threw caution to the winds, drove down the hill and pulled up directly opposite the first of the cottages. There was a number 1 on its gate-post. He put the car into first gear and crawled forward, past the other cottages and the man who had now finished mowing his grass and was hoeing the flower-beds around it. Number 8, at the end of the row, was as spick and span as the rest but showed no signs of life.

Sod it, thought Harry, becoming impatient with his own indecision. He slammed the car door behind him, walked up the path and rang the bell.

Nothing happened. He rang it again, then went and peered in through the window. The room inside looked lived-in, with a newspaper strewn across the arm of a chair and some torn-open envelopes on the table, but with no sign of whoever might be living there.

He went back to his car, knowing he was being watched by the man in the straw hat. No point in hanging about. He would go back into Palmer's Heath, get some lunch and try again later.

He was heading back to the pub when he saw the Grange

with its fête now in full swing and remembered what the landlord had said about it being the place where everyone would be. No doubt 'everyone' meant locals leading blameless lives and not the kind of desperado Harry was after. Still, it was worth a try. He turned in at the gates and was waved on to the end of a line of parked cars.

Quite what the fête was in aid of he never found out. There were women selling cakes and jars of jam, piles of second-hand books and then a small display of silver jewellery arranged on green baize. An elderly man was selling pot-plants next to a young woman who was sitting on the grass with a display of water-colours around her. On another stall Harry was persuaded to buy a tombola ticket and, to his dismay, found himself presented with a bottle of dandelion wine. 'No, it's all right. You keep it,' he urged, but in vain; he had paid for the ticket and the prize was rightfully his. In the end he carried away the bottle and dropped it into a clump of rhododendron bushes.

He resisted an invitation to throw darts for goldfish for fear he might win again and have to dump the luckless creature alongside the dandelion wine and he forced himself, instead, to concentrate on the faces around him. He was, after all, there on dangerous business which might yet backfire if his adversary should catch first sight of him. Watching the families passing, with their baby-buggies and dogs he felt himself as much a tourist as he had in Spain. This was the England that had carried on, secure in its own identity, while the cities and industrial towns had changed and decayed.

He soon found he'd covered the whole garden and was back at his starting-point, having seen everything but the one face for which he was looking. He had also, in the course of his travels, located the beer tent, a small marquee with one flap raised where men were standing in small groups and talking quietly. He'd intended to go in search of food, but the thought of a quick drink on what was turning out to be a warm and, so far, fruitless day suddenly had its attractions. He wandered over and ducked under the furled canvas. Inside was a small, makeshift bar with its metal canisters of beer standing beside it. Harry ordered a pint and then winced, seeing the white plastic beaker in which it was being served. Don't be such a bloody purist, he told himself, what does it matter what it's in so long as it tastes as it should?

Suddenly none of it mattered. He glimpsed the profile of a man to his left, a man standing alone, not more than five paces away and engrossed in a folded newspaper. It set his heart pounding with excitement. For here, at last, was the face he'd been seeking, a face he'd last seen in Spain. It was proof of everything Eric Buller had told him. More importantly, it would allow him to confirm his suspicions about Rebecca's death.

He paid for his beakerful of beer, trying to work out what to do for the best. All he knew for sure was that he had to confront the other man. After that he might talk to Porterhouse or the Yard, but first there was the personal score to settle. He moved quietly across till he was standing beside him.

'Well, hello,' he said. 'And how're you, then, Norris?'

'Shit.'

Norris stared at him, open-mouthed. Harry observed with interest his attempts to change his appearance. He had grown a small neat moustache. And surely his hair had been mousier before, not so blond? But none of it altered the basic contours of the face nor stopped this being Norris Edgerton, back from the dead and looking remarkably well on it.

'Surprise, surprise,' said Harry.

Norris looked round in alarm, as if expecting to be attacked. Then, when nothing happened, he licked his lips and said, 'What the fuck are you doing here?'

'Looking for you.'

'Yes?' he eyed him, looked round again, then gave a short, desperate laugh. 'Jesus.'

'I've been up to your house,' said Harry evenly. 'Found nobody there, so I came down here.'

'My house . . . ?'

'Well, your wife's, then. Where do you live? You live somewhere else?'

Norris glanced around again, as if he still couldn't believe Harry was alone and there wasn't a dragnet of police waiting to pounce. 'No, I, er . . . I live there all right. But I'm generally regarded as the boy-friend, see. Back from the oil-rigs.'

'I see.'

'Got a new name and everything.'

'What's that?'

'Dave Seymour.'

'It suits you.'

'Thanks.'

'And there's nobody here knows you of old?'

'No. We'd only bought the cottage a couple of weeks before I had to high-tail it for Spain. So Lesley moved in by herself and let on she was divorced.' He was beginning to relax. 'Who else knows?' he asked.

'Knows what?'

'About me? 'Bout me being still alive and not . . . well, not dead.'

'Nobody.'

'What, you mean . . . just you?'

'Just me,' said Harry.

Norris nodded, relieved. 'And how did you manage to work it out?'

'I didn't. Not till I had a talk with Eric Buller.'

'Eric . . . ?' Clearly the name didn't mean much.

'The dentist,' said Harry. 'Well, he was a dentist. Till he got struck off for fiddling the Natinal Health.'

'Oh.' Norris nodded. 'Him. Yes. He's been talking, has he?'

'Only to me.'

No point in explaining how, off her own bat, Yvonne had come up with the recent and sad history of Eric Buller, BDS, LDS, who had sought to enlarge the profits of his thriving practice by falsifying his National Health returns, got found out and been prosecuted. The fine had been enormous, but an even greater blow was the action of the British Dental Association in

170

barring him from further practice *sine die*. The financial consequences had been swift. He'd been forced to sell his Dulwich house, saying goodbye to his next-door neighbour, Leo Shapiro, and done a quick flit to Caledonian Road, Slough. For which his wife had never forgiven him.

Norris, too, seemed to regard himself as betrayed.

'There's always somebody, isn't there? Always some bleeder you can't trust to keep his mouth shut.'

'I shouldn't hold it against him,' said Harry. 'I more or less conned him into talking.'

Norris gave a grunt, still dissatisfied. 'He was paid for not talking. Either to you or anybody else.'

'So tell me,' said Harry, 'what exactly did happen to Tommy Smith?'

'You want to know?'

'I do.'

Norris shrugged and said, 'What happened to Tommy was that he got pissed, fell in his own swimming-pool and drowned. Like me really, only the main difference was that he did it for real. Me, I was just pretending.'

Harry wanted it spelling out. 'So you staged your own death so's it'd be identical to Tommy's. And then you swapped his body for yours?'

'Exactly.'

'Why?'

'Why?' echoed Norris, and gave a hollow laugh. 'You want to know why?'

'Only if you want to tell me.'

He considered it, then said, 'Why not? The reason why was that I had to get out somehow. I mean I had to. I couldn't spend the rest of my natural rotting over there. Worse than being in the nick.'

'You were home-sick?'

'Call it that if you like. I'll tell you what I was sick of. I was sick of the fucking sun. I couldn't stand another four years of that. And, anyway, let's be honest, the future out there wasn't looking too rosy, what with everybody talking about extradition and such-like. I mean the bleeders never wanted us over there in the first place, so you can bet they'd be happy to see the back of us once they'd got the legislation to do it. I mean, you know as well as I do – they weren't too concerned about my death, were they?'

'Not a lot,' admitted Harry.

They might have been a pair of old mates reminiscing, save that each remained wary of the other. Harry was still angling for confirmation of what he was already ninety-nine per cent sure – that Norris had not only stage-managed his own death but had, more violently, engineered Rebecca's. For his part, Norris was clearly waiting for Harry to show his hand; just how much did he know and why had he come seeking him? It was a patient battle of wits, kept that way by the beer tent and the people around them.

'When Tommy Smith died,' said Harry, 'who found him?'

'Me.'

'By yourself?'

'Yes. I called by one night at a bit of a loose end. And there he was, floating about like some great bloody whale.'

'What did you do?'

'Called Natras. The coloured guy that has the clinic. I believe you've met him, according to what my missus tells me.'

'Yes.'

'Well, I called him. 'Cause I'd met him before and I could see as soon as I set eyes on him he was out for what he could get. I mean, some people you can just tell that, can't you? Almost smell it coming off 'em.'

'So you'd already had the idea of substituting Tommy Smith's body for yours?'

'Yes. Had that idea five minutes after I fished poor old Tommy out. It was just a matter of squaring it. Cost me a bob or two, I can tell you.'

'You bribed Natras?'

Norris nodded. 'He's got expensive tastes, so it wasn't too difficult. He's into yachts and all that. I think with what I've given him he should be able to buy the fucking *Britannia*.'

172

'Who else was in on it?'

'Just Gerald and Alan. They was happy to help 'cause they was neither of 'em too flush. Most of what they'd come over with they'd already spent, and they're going to need every penny they can get their hands on if that extradition business ever gets under way.'

'OK,' said Harry. 'So what happened? You kept Tommy Smith's body . . . ?'

'The doc did,' Norris corrected him. 'All tucked up nice and cold while I got things sorted.'

'Like Eric Buller.'

'Definitely. See, I reckoned Tommy could pass for me for all practical purposes. We're about the same age and build. The only people who'd notice the difference was being paid to keep their mouths shut. We reckoned on the police not being too interested. And then the only other person who was going to turn up and expect to see the body was the wife. Who, of course, knew all about what was going on anyway.'

'And Scotland Yard,' Harry reminded him.

'Ah yes. They was the problem. I didn't know what they might get up to by way of wanting to identify the body and suchlike. So I had a word with our mutual friend, Mr Shapiro.'

'Who happened to know a dodgy dentist.'

'He knows a lot of people, does Leo. That's why he is where he is.'

'I'm sure.'

'Anyhow, we reckoned that, if they was in any doubt . . . This is Scotland Yard I'm talking about . . . '

'Yes.'

'If they was in any doubt then they'd rely on the old dental records routine. Which was what they did. Went over and took X-rays. Only, of course, Mr Buller, or whatever he was called, had already been over and shoved in a few fillings here and whipped out a couple of molars there so that Tommy's mouth would come out looking like mine.'

'Clever stuff,' said Harry wryly. 'You know Leo employed me to find him?'

'I did gather something of the sort, yes. For which I'm very grateful.'

Harry restrained himself from responding and just said, 'Go on.'

'Well, you know the rest 'cause you was there at the time. We set up the party so's everybody could see I was getting pissed out of my head, which, of course, I wasn't, not really. Then, when everybody had gone home, the doc arrived with Tommy's body, and I set out for the airport with a passport I'd had done special, again with a little assistance from Leo. And I'm at home having breakfast by the time the hue-and-cry's started over there. Not a bad bit of planning, even if I do say so myself.'

He gave a little chuckle and looked to see whether Harry was also entertained by the account.

'Then you killed Rebecca,' said Harry flatly.

Norris took a step back, as though to avoid the accusation. 'You what?'

'You killed Rebecca.'

'I did no such bloody thing.'

'Yes,' insisted Harry quietly.

'You think I . . . ? Come off it, Harry boy. What would I want to do a thing like that for?'

'Because she found out. She charmed some Spanish tax lawyer into sticking his nose into your financial affairs, and he found out about the money you'd withdrawn to make the payments to Natras and to Fieldhouse and Mullins.'

'Balls. Why should she have been interested anyway? What was it to do with her?'

'She was curious.'

'She was what?' he said, now openly scornful.

'She thought there was something wrong about the way you were acting. And she believed you when you fed her a line about Tommy Smith's disappearance. How there was something mysterious about that. So, when you were supposed to have died accidentally, she thought there was something mysterious about that as well. First of all she got me to ask questions; then, when I got nowhere, she started asking 'em herself.'

Norris gave a snort of contempt and shook his head. 'Look, we can't talk here,' he said, dropping his empty beaker on to the grass. 'Let's go . . . ' He waved vaguely at the gardens outside the marquee. 'Well, at least let's get out of this bloody tent.'

With no option but to follow him, Harry placed his almost untouched drink on the bar, and they walked out together into the sunlight. He wondered whether Norris really was looking for somewhere they could talk more privately or whether there was some darker plan behind this move. For himself, he had to let events take their course till he had the confirmation he needed.

'We might get some peace and quiet over there,' said Norris, and he walked determinedly towards the house, then veered off so that their course was taking them past it. They crossed a cobbled yard with unused stables on one side and out-houses on the other.

There was no one about. Suddenly they had escaped from the ruck of the fête and were quite alone, their footsteps sounding on the cobbles. Norris led them through an arched gateway, and they were at the back of the house where the gardens, away from public view, were less carefully tended.

'Seems quiet enough,' said Norris, looking round.

He was pretending, Harry realised. The air of aimlessness was intended to deceive. He'd known about this place before-hand and brought them both to it for a purpose.

'You seem to know your way around,' said Harry.

'Been casing the joint,' said Norris, and grinned. 'Well, not seriously. Just had a wander round earlier this morning. I mean, look at it. Bloody great place like this. No alarms, no dogs. They're begging for it.'

They came to a vegetable garden, with its pyramids of canes, and then a greenhouse and flower-beds set out with seedlings. Then, beyond a screen of young conifers, they came to a paved area in the middle of which, to Harry's surprise, was a small swimming-pool, empty of water. Its pale blue tiles, chipped here and there, were littered with old leaves which in a corner of the deep end had drifted to a mouldering heap.

Norris stopped and turned to face him. 'OK, Harry boy, let's stop pissing about. How much do you want?'

Harry shook his head. 'Not a penny.'

'Well, I think you should. I mean why not? All the other buggers got their cut. You found the dentist when we needed the talkative bastard. Then you went over there yourself and provided an extra witness, which was probably no bad thing. I mean looking at it from your point-of-view, I can see you might think you deserve something for all the trouble and inconvenience. I can see all that. You're entitled. So – how much?'

'That's not why I'm here.'

Norris sighed. 'All right, that's not why you're here. But I *want* to give you something. I *want* to, all right? On account of you've found out my little secret and I want you to keep quiet about it. And naturally that's something I'm willing to pay for. Be very wrong if I wasn't.'

'Tell me about Rebecca,' said Harry.

'Jesus Christ . . . !'

'You killed her.'

Norris raised a warning finger as though to jab at Harry with it, but stopped within an inch of his chest. 'I thought I'd already said. I know nothing about that.'

'Well, I think you do. I think you know everything about it.'

'You're a very brave man, Harry boy. You know that? Also very stupid.'

They stood facing one another, Harry slightly the taller, Norris broader and heavier. Only the faintest of cries reached them from the other side of the house. A cat stalked by on the far side of the empty pool but paid them no attention.

'You fancied her, did you?' taunted Norris. 'Is that what this is all about? You fancied the pants off her? Or perhaps you had 'em off her . . . ?'

'Why did you have to do it?' said Harry. 'Why kill her?'

'You're asking for trouble, you know that?'

'I'll tell you what I think.'

176

'Don't bother.'

'I think she worked out what had happened. Perhaps went to Doctor Natras and got him to admit to it. Or Mullins and Fieldhouse, one of them, I don't know.'

'No, well, you don't know very much, do you?'

'Then she came over here. Because she wanted to tell me I'd been wrong in not listening to her when she knew there was something dodgy about your accidental death. And I daresay she had a few things she wanted to say to you as well.'

'Like what?'

'Well, you saw her so you know that better than I do.'

'No,' said Norris stubbornly.

'But if you want me to make a guess then I'd guess she thought it was pretty lousy the way you'd set her up along with the rest of us.'

'Crap.'

Harry ploughed on. 'She called at my office, but I wasn't there. So she left a number for me to phone and went back to her hotel. From where she made a couple of calls herself. One of them was to you.'

'You know, I ought to knock your fucking head off,' muttered Norris.

'Perhaps you'd told her where your wife lived. Or anyway she found out. It was easy for me, so it would have been just as easy for her. She rang, and you answered the phone. You told her to stay where she was and then went to see her.'

'You've got witnesses for this? You've got evidence?'

'And when you got there, she told you what a shit you were for making a fool out of her. Treating her as though she was on the other side instead of yours. And you warned her to keep her mouth shut. Which she didn't like. And so you threatened her. Which she liked even less. So you ended up killing her.'

Norris opened his mouth to reply, then stopped as his eyes went over Harry's left shoulder and registered alarm at what he saw. Harry turned instinctively to see what it was and knew instantly, a split second too late, that he'd been suckered.

Norris's punch was low, driven into his stomach. He doubled

over, gasping with pain and shock. Then came a kick which caught him on the side of his head with shuddering force. For a moment he knew nothing, then consciousness returned. He was on the ground, raising an arm and bringing up his knees to protect himself.

He also knew he'd been right. Norris had killed her. The assault was as good as a signed confession.

He saw Norris pulling something from the bushes a few feet away. It was an iron bar, which he raised above his head. Harry rolled sideways, but Norris, instead of bringing the weapon down and smashing the ground where his head had been, only followed him and re-aligned himself for the blow. Harry threw himself into another, even more desperate spin and was suddenly falling. He landed on a hard, unyielding surface with a force that winded him and sent shock-waves of pain through his body. He had rolled over the side and fallen to the bottom of the empty pool.

14.

It was a drop of four or five feet, nearer to the shallow than the deep end. Norris jumped down after him but landed clumsily and staggered to regain his balance. It gave Harry the chance to scramble to his feet and move out of range, thankful he didn't seem seriously injured. Though Norris, now coming after him, was out to change that.

They circled one another like bears in a pit. Norris swung the bar. Harry swayed back, avoiding it. Norris advanced, driving Harry before him towards the deep end. Harry sensed the tiled wall at his back and knew he was close to being trapped. Needing to make his move, he feigned attack, provoking Norris to take another swing at him with the bar, then, when the blow had passed, Harry leaped at him.

He managed to get a grip on Norris's arm, which at least prevented him trying to bash his brains out with the iron bar again, then they were grappling, grunting with effort as each strained to topple the other. It wasn't Harry's kind of fight, this heavyweight wrestling. Though the fitter of the two men, he felt himself being overwhelmed by the other's bulk. He got a hand on the iron bar, then found he was close to being throttled by it. Norris had hold of both ends and was pulling it in towards Harry's neck. Harry struggled to hold it off and it became a trial of strength between them.

Seeing he was in danger of losing it, he stamped down hard on Norris's toes. Norris, wearing only trainers, gave a yell of pain, which was cut short by an elbow to his stomach. He lost his grip on the bar, and Harry was able to tug it free, though without getting a real grasp on it himself, so that it fell to the ground between them.

Norris bent to retrieve it. Harry, able at last to use his fists in the way he knew, landed a punch to his face

179

that sent him reeling away.

Kicking the bar aside, he went after Norris, hammering at him with both fists. Norris tried at first to retaliate but his blows were wild and easily evaded. He was taking a painful battering and seemed suddenly to realise it, for he turned and ran towards the shallow end where he might more easily pull himself out.

Harry raced after him and caught him as he heaved himself up on to the side. There was a moment's mad activity as Norris, half in and half out of the pool, kicked out backwards with both feet. Finally Harry managed to grab one of the flailing legs and yanked down on it. It broke Norris's grip on the edge. He slid down, and there was a sharp crack as his head connected with the stone rim. His eyes rolled upwards, then his eyelids closed and he collapsed unconscious at Harry's feet.

Once sure that Norris wasn't going to be moving for some time, Harry took a moment to get his own breath back and calm himself. What he needed now was some way of immobilising Norris. He gazed round and decided the greenhouse was the best bet. He stepped over Norris and pulled himself out of the pool. Now the adrenalin had stopped pumping, his body had become a mass of aches and pains. Nothing broken so far as he could tell, but every part of him had begun to ache, each in a quite distinctive way.

The greenhouse offered the choice of a coiled hose-pipe, a ball of garden twine or a length of old clothes-line. Harry took both the twine and the clothes-line and went back to where Norris hadn't even stirred. He found the business of tying him up awkward and laborious. His own fingers were sore from the fight and moving the unconscious body to get the rope beneath it was back-breaking work. Eventually, though, he had him well and truly trussed, with clothes-line and twine criss-crossing his body and pulling tight across his stomach as he breathed.

Harry's next need was for a phone. He'd already decided the house offered the best chance of that. He left Norris lying on the bottom of the pool and approached the back door.

Not surprisingly it was locked. But, as Norris had pointed out, the security wasn't too clever, and the lock was a simple Yale. Harry took out his special credit card, the one long out-of-date he carried for eventualities such as this, and slipped it between the jamb and the door. Then came some patient trial-and-error till he was able to spring the lock and push the door open.

It admitted him to a scullery, which had freezers and washing-machines and a row of wellingtons in different sizes. He listened a moment, but there was no sound from within, only the distant, jolly din of the fête coming from the far side of the house. So he stepped cautiously through the scullery and came into a much larger kitchen which, as well as a long pine table and an Aga cooker, held the telephone he was looking for. It was mounted on the wall, with a clip-board full of scribbled messages beside it.

He dialled 999 and asked for Police.

'Police. How can I help you?'

'Listen carefully. I'm going to tell you where you'll find Norris Edgerton. Have you got that? Norris Edgerton.'

'And what's your name, caller?'

'Never mind my name. Norris Edgerton, that's the only name you need to remember.'

'We must have your name, caller.'

'He's a well-known villain. Scotland Yard'll be interested in him, even if you aren't.'

'What's your number then, caller?'

'Norris Edgerton, right? He's supposed to have died in Spain a few weeks ago, but that was all a put-up job. He's alive and he's in Palmer's Heath. You know Palmer's Heath?'

'Yes.'

'There's a big house called the Grange. I don't know the address but it's a bloody enormous place and there's a fête on just now so you can't miss it.'

'Is that where you are?'

181

'That's where Norris Edgerton is. There's a swimming-pool behind the house. He's in that.'

'He's in . . . what?'

'Oh, don't worry. The pool's empty. It's an empty swimming-pool. He's tied up and he's in there, right?'

'And he's called what? Norris Edgerton . . . ?'

'For Christ's sake . . . Norris Edgerton, yes. And he's at the Grange. Palmer's Heath. He's tied up in an empty swimming-pool.'

'And what did you say your name was?'

'I didn't. And listen. The week before last there was a woman killed in a London hotel. She was called Rebecca Connors. Rebecca Connors, right? Well, the man in the swimming-pool – he killed her.'

And he put down the receiver.

He went back to check on Norris and found he'd regained consciousness. His eyes were open and staring up at him.

'Don't worry,' said Harry. 'Police shouldn't be too long.'

'I'll pay you,' muttered Norris through swollen lips. 'Name it. Anything.'

Harry laughed. 'No chance.'

'Bastard.'

Harry laughed again. Norris began to writhe, straining against the cords binding him, but the only effect was to pull them tighter. Harry waited long enough to see they would hold, then turned and walked away. As he crossed the cobbled yard at the side of the house, he heard the sound of approaching sirens.

The fête was still going strong, and he wondered about a drink in the beer tent, this time by way of celebration. But the first people he passed turned to stare. He looked down and saw his clothes were stained from the struggle. He tried to flatten his hair and wondered whether his face was marked. Better to slip away quietly. He might be conspicuous in the beer tent, especially when the police started asking questions.

They were here now, a car weaving its way up the drive and drawing curious glances. With more to come, to judge from the sound of approaching sirens.

Harry watched the police-car pass, then hurried to his own car. He would have his drink in comfort, back at the flat. Besides, Jill would be there waiting for him.

'I know,' he said as he entered to where she was sitting on the sofa. 'I look a mess. I know I do.'

She stared. 'Harry . . . ? What . . . what's happened?'

'Don't worry. I'll tell you all about it.'

'But are you all right?'

'Great. Never better.'

It reassured him to see her concern. Though he also noticed, as no doubt he was meant to, her suitcase still packed and standing on the floor beside her.

'Do you want a drink?'

'Not . . . not now, no.'

'Well, I do.'

He poured himself a whisky, then gently, out of respect for his bruises, lowered himself into a chair.

'But what's happened?' she asked.

'Oh, just been tying up a few loose ends. Like I say, I'll tell you about it later. But what about you? What's been happening to you?'

He saw she'd been smoking again. The ashtray at her elbow contained two stubs.

'I'm fine,' she said, drawing back as if regretting her instinctive show of concern for him. 'I just don't know what to do, that's all.'

'About what?'

'About us.'

'No problem. Move back in. Now. Go and unpack, and I'll take you out to celebrate.'

Suddenly, and for the first time in their relationship, he felt himself the stronger and more secure of the two. Despite her determination to stay distant and detached, he knew she didn't want to leave him and so was here hoping to hear him say the right things – whatever they were – that would allow her to move back in.

'It's not as easy as that,' she said.

'Why not?'

She took a breath and, without looking at him, embarked on what had the ring of a prepared speech about it.

'I have to be able to trust you, Harry. I know what it's like to live with a man I can't trust, a man who lies to me. I've done that before and I don't want to have to go through it again. If I'm to stay, then I have to be able to trust you.'

'Sure,' he said, and went to pour himself another whisky.

'Which I thought I could.'

'You can. Of course you can.'

She remained silent till he sat down again, then said, 'Then will you tell me the truth about Rebecca? The girl we met in Spain? Oh, I know she was killed in a horrible fashion, but I still have to know, Harry. I have to know what happened between you.'

So that was it. Well, he could hardly claim it was a surprise. He had known all along of the unhappiness she was nursing but had preferred to ignore it. Hoping without any real hope that his fling with poor Rebecca had gone unnoticed and so wouldn't have any repercussions.

'Please, Harry, just tell me the truth. I don't mind what it is but I need to know it.'

He nodded. After all, why should he tell her? Rebecca was dead, and so Jill could hardly suspect a continuing relationship. If she felt she had to know what happened in Spain, then she should be told.

'You want to know whether we had an affair?'

'Yes.'

He downed the rest of his whisky and looked her in the eye, seeing her fear of what he was about to confess.

'Well, the truth,' he said, 'is that we didn't have any affair. We were never lovers. Just friends, that's all.'

'Oh, Harry,' she cried, her face alight with relief. 'Oh, thank

184

God. Because – I can tell you now – I really couldn't have stayed if you'd had an affair with her. I really couldn't.'

'Well, I didn't,' he lied. 'And that's the truth.'

She left the sofa and threw herself into his bruised arms.

If you have enjoyed this book and would like to receive details of other Walker Adventure titles, please write to:

Adventure Editor
Walker and Company
720 Fifth Avenue
New York, NY 10019